CHARMING A CHRISTMAS TEXAN
Copyright © 2022 by Katie Lane

All rights reserved. Except for use in any review, the reproduction or utilization of this work in whole or in part in any form by any electronic, mechanical or other means, now known or hereinafter invented, including xerography, photocopying and recording, or in any information storage or retrieval system, is forbidden without the written permission of the publisher.

This book is a work of fiction. Names, characters, places, and incidents are a product of the writer's imagination. All rights reserved. Scanning, uploading, and electronic sharing of this book without the permission of the author is unlawful piracy and theft. To obtain permission to excerpt portions of the text, please contact the author at katie@katielanebooks.com Thank you for respecting this author's hard work and livelihood.

Cover Design and Interior Format
© KILLION

# Charming a

## CHRISTMAS TEXAN

KINGMAN
RANCH
· 6 ·

# KATIE LANE

*To all those peeps who LOVE a
holiday happily ever after.
I hope this one warms your heart like
a cup of hot cocoa.*

# CHAPTER ONE

WEDDING RECEPTIONS WERE the perfect settings for bad choices.

Not that Everly Grayson had ever made good ones. Her choices in life had always leaned toward the bad. Which is how she ended up quitting high school and running away to Dallas to become a tattoo artist. Falling head over heels in love with her best friend. And managing a bar in a Podunk Texas town when she hated small towns with a passion.

But last night at Buck and Mystic Kingman's wedding reception she had taken her bad decision-making one step further.

Everly stared at the man lying in bed next to her. His features were identical to his twin brother's. But she had always been able to tell the two apart. Mostly because Chance Ransom scowled whenever she was around.

He wasn't scowling now. His face was relaxed in sleep, his lips slightly parted and emitting a huff of air on each exhalation. His sandy locks were usually styled back from his face with not a hair out of place. This morning, the thick strands shot up in spiky tufts that softened his stern features and gave him a boyish look.

Although there was nothing boyish about the dark stubble that covered his strong jaw.

Everly had always loved a little stubble. She liked the way it looked and she liked the way it felt against her skin when a man's face was right between her—

*Hell no, Everly James Grayson. Don't you dare let your libido take charge like you did last night. You already made a mistake. You don't need to compound it.*

She reached over and shook Chance awake. "Time to rise and shine."

Chance's long lashes slowly opened. The early morning light coming in the window must have been too much for him because he cringed and slammed his eyes shut again. She figured he had one helluva of a hangover. Her head pounded and she hadn't downed half as much wedding punch as Chance had.

What the hell had been in that punch?

Chance massaged his temples and groaned. "Good Lord."

"I don't know if the Lord had anything to do with last night," she said.

With a jerk of his head, Chance turned to her. She'd thought his eyes were the same soft brown as Shane's. But this close, she realized that there was nothing soft about Chance's eyes. The pupils were hard onyx surrounded by a ring of steamy coffee. The mixture was deep, dark . . . and sexy. They held surprise for a split second and then horror, like she was the worst possible nightmare he'd ever had.

She figured to a pastor, she was.

She grinned. "Good mornin', Preach."

He continued to stare at her. "What are you doing in my bed?"

She stretched her arms over her head and yawned loudly. "I think that should be my question, Goldilocks."

He sat straight up, cringing from the pain that no doubt ricocheted through his head. He looked around the room and then back at her before he covered his face with both his hands and muttered, "What have I done?"

She was feeling the same way. But she had never been someone who spent a lot of time on regret.

"Now, Preach," she said. "It's not a big deal. All people sin from time to time. Even holier-than-thou preachers. I'm sure God will forgive you for one night of debauchery."

He lowered his hands and stared at her. "Debauchery?"

"Well, maybe not debauchery as much as a little wicked fun. And there's nothing wrong with a little wicked fun." Everly reached out and patted his forearm.

It was hard not to notice the flex of muscles beneath her palm . . . or the ones stacked up his stomach to his chest like building blocks. Chance's physique had surprised her. She'd thought a preacher's body would be pale from lack of sun and puny from lack of exercise. But she'd been way off base. A caramel tan covered defined pectorals, biceps, and two rows of tummy muscles. Shane had a nice body, but if Everly was honest—and she was always honest—Chance's wasn't just nice. It was . . . lickable.

Not that she had licked it. Or that she would ever lick it. But last night, eating him like salted caramel frozen yogurt had crossed her mind.

Her gaze slid over his chest . . . and it was still crossing her mind.

Chance uttered a very un-preacher like curse beneath his breath and jumped out of bed.

Or tried to.

The sheet caught around his feet and he almost took a header to the floor. He kicked free and got up. She tried to look away—okay, maybe she didn't try that hard. Speaking of hard. She got a glimpse of a great ass and an impressive morning erection before he grabbed the sheet and wrapped it around his waist.

He stared at her. "Tell me what happened."

She fluffed the pillows and reclined back on them, uncaring of where the sheet settled. Chance's gaze lowered to her bare stomach for a brief second before it quickly lifted. The annoyance in his eyes was easy to read. He obviously didn't like the shorty tank top she slept in. Or maybe it was her belly button ring that ticked him off. Whatever it was, she refused to let his censorship make her feel inferior.

"You should've seen the piercing I had in my nose. I hated to get rid of it, but it kept getting caked with boogers."

His censorious look grew. "Do you have to share everything?"

She shrugged. "I thought the Bible says, 'The truth will set you free.'"

"Jesus wasn't talking about telling everyone your personal information. He was talking about the truth of the word of God. If you know God's truth, it will set you free."

She studied him. "Hmm? You know God's word and you don't seem very free. In fact, you seem as tense as a clock that has been wound too tightly and needs to be sprung in order to keep ticking." She laughed. "And it looks like all you needed was a little spiked punch to get sprung."

"It's not funny." He ran a hand through his hair and looked around as if searching for help. "What happened last night was wrong. All wrong. I shouldn't have even attended the reception. I shouldn't have accepted the cup of punch. Or any of the ones after. And I certainly shouldn't have gone to bed . . . " He glanced back at her. "With you."

The entire scenario of a Ransom twin telling her what a mistake he'd made by sleeping with her was like déjà vu. Shane might have been a lot nicer with his rejection after their night of drunken college sex, but the message was the same—Everly wasn't the girl they wanted to find in their beds the following morning. Suddenly, she wasn't having fun anymore prodding the preacher. So she decided to let him off the hook.

"Well, you certainly aren't my first choice

either, Preach. So I guess we're both lucky that nothing happened last night."

He stared at her suspiciously. "Then why am I naked?"

"Because you stripped off all your clothes before you passed out in my bed. I found you after I closed up the bar."

"And you joined me instead of trying to wake me up?"

"I was a little tipsy myself. Not to mention exhausted from pouring drinks all night for the entire town. Walking down the hall to the other room seemed like too much trouble. Besides, it's my bed. You were the interloper. And what did you want me to do? Send you home falling-down drunk? If I had let the new preacher get run over or stumble and crack open his head, the town would tar and feather me. If word gets out that Nasty Jack's tattooed bartender lured you into her bed, they still might."

She saw the strong need to believe her in his eyes. Finally, his shoulders relaxed and he released his breath. "Thank God." Holding the sheet like a shy virgin, he picked up his clothing scattered over the floor and walked out of the room. A few seconds later, she heard the bathroom door slam shut.

She blew out her breath and rubbed her aching temples. "Way to go, Everly. You just couldn't learn your lesson the first time, could you?"

The toilet flushed, making her realize how badly she had to go. She got up and searched for her jeans. Once she pulled them on, she headed downstairs.

Nasty Jack's was a typical small town Texas honky-tonk. It had a well-worn pool table, a bootheel-scarred dance floor, an old .45 jukebox, a bunch of mismatched tables and chairs, and a long bar that covered one entire wall. Christmas lights hung year round above the bar and classic beer signs glowed from the walls.

The only thing that made Nasty Jack's different from most small town bars was the pie. The owner's wife made them from scratch and Gretchen Kingman knew how to bake a pie. The short time Everly had managed the bar, she had become addicted to the tasty treat. There was something about the flaky crust and gooey fillings that made her feel better about her bad life choices.

So after using the women's bathroom, she headed to the kitchen in search of some pie comfort. She found half of a raspberry peach pie hidden beneath a dishtowel. After making a strong pot of coffee—another addiction—she poured herself a mugful, grabbed a fork, and sat down at the prep island to indulge.

As she ate, her thoughts drifted back to the preacher ... something that had been happening a lot lately. He was as different from his brother as night and day. Shane wore all his emotions on his sleeve while Chance seemed to hide all his behind the fake smile he gave his entire congregation. Having grown up with phony parents, Everly could spot a fake a mile away. Of course, it didn't hurt that she knew the story behind Chance's fake smile.

The sound of clicking bootheels drew her attention away from her thoughts. She figured Chance would sneak out the door without a word. So she was surprised when he walked in through the swinging door.

Damn, she loved a man in a Stetson. The brown felt of his hat matched his eyes and made them even more intense. But the rest of him looked pretty pathetic. His dress shirt and pants were covered in wrinkles and the skin under his dark stubble had a grayish tinge. Like a true Texas gentlemen, he removed his hat when he reached her. His sandy hair still stuck up in boyish tufts and Everly had to stifle the urge to reach out and ruffle it even more.

He cleared his throat. "I owe you an apology, Everly. I shouldn't have assumed you were responsible for me being in your bed."

She took the last bite of pie and shrugged. "No sweat, Preach. I've had worse assumptions made about me."

"Well, I was wrong. And I'd appreciate it if you didn't . . ." He let the sentence drift off, but she knew what he was asking.

She mimed zipping her lips. "My lips are sealed as tight as my grandmother's fruitcake." She glanced up at the ceiling. "God rest her soul. Grandma wrapped that cake in so many layers of plastic wrap it took you from Thanksgiving to Christmas just to get into it. Not that it was worth the trouble." She shivered. "Worst cake you'd ever eat in your life."

"Well, thank you for not saying anything to anyone about last night."

"No problem. Although you're still going to be the subject of gossip." She sent him a saucy smile. "I don't think the town realized how well their new preacher could dance."

He stared at her. "I danced?"

"A lot. You even dipped Miss Kitty."

Chance rubbed his temples and groaned. "I'm sure the church board is already planning a meeting to fire me."

"Doubtful. If they didn't fire you for punching a Kingman—and we all know how much they worship the Kingmans—I doubt they'll fire you for doing a little drinking and dancing at a wedding."

Everly had been at the bar fight between the Ransom brothers and the Kingman brothers. Wolfe Kingman had been about to rough Shane up for breaking Delaney's heart when Chance appeared out of nowhere and started throwing punches. It had surprised everyone. Everly included. She had thought preachers believed in turning the other cheek. Obviously, not when it concerned their family.

"They should fire me," Chance said. His face held guilt and the deep pain it always held. It was the pain that got to her.

"Don't be so hard on yourself. You were just enjoying a wedding reception like everyone else in town."

His eyes narrowed. "Except for you. If I remember correctly, you weren't enjoying the reception."

"I was bartending."

His gaze grew more intent. "And watching Shane."

It was more than a little annoying that he couldn't seem to remember what they had done last night, but he had no trouble remembering other details. Details she'd just as soon forget.

She shrugged. "What can I say? Shane is a good dancer. Did you two take lessons when you were kids?"

He didn't fall for the subject change. "Give it up, Everly. Shane is happy."

The pie in her stomach threatened to come back up. She pushed the metal pie plate away and took a sip of coffee before she spoke. "You don't have to tell me. I know your brother is happy." She knew it all too well.

"Do you?" He set his hand on the stainless-steel island and leaned closer. "Then why did you take the job here in Cursed, Everly? With your business degree and experience managing restaurants, you could have easily found a managerial position anywhere. Why here?"

"Wolfe and Gretchen Kingman needed help. What can I say? I'm a giving person."

Chance shook his head. "That wasn't the reason. The real reason is that you're still not over my brother. And you think if you hang out long enough in Cursed, Shane will realize what a mistake he made marrying Delaney and come running back to you."

She snorted. "Wow, you have some imagination, Preach. I'm not still pining for Shane."

"Really? What color shirt did he have on last night?"

As much as she didn't want to know, she did. Green-and-yellow plaid with a touch of baby blue. She got up on shaky legs that didn't feel like they could support her. But Everly had always been good at beating the odds.

Except for love.

Those odds had beaten her soundly.

She forced a smile. "Sorry to cut you off, Preach, but I've got better things to do on my day off than listen to a sermon from the town pastor."

She went to sweep past him, but his hand shot out and grabbed her arm. His dark eyes glittered with warning. "Shane is never going to leave Delaney for you, Everly. I'll make sure of it. So go home to Dallas. There's nothing for you in Cursed."

# Chapter Two

"WHO ARE YOU?"

Chance stared at the man in the mirror.

His eyes were bloodshot with dark circles beneath. His face had a pale, sickly tinge and two razor nicks. And his lips were pressed in a thin, firm line of pain. Pain that had nothing to do with the throbbing behind his temples or the rolling of his stomach. This was a deeper pain—the pain of loss that grew from the depths of your soul, entwining you in its tentacles and squeezing until you couldn't breathe.

Instead of answering the question, the man just continued to stare back at him with a haunted look. Turning from the mirror with disgust, Chance headed into the bedroom to get dressed.

He had always been an orderly person. Ever since he was young, he had liked having everything in its place. As a child, his side of the room he shared with Shane had been organized and neat. Now his bedroom was a jumbled mess. Half-unpacked boxes were everywhere and he had to search through a pile of unfolded laundry to find clean underwear and socks. His closet was even worse. Suit jackets, pants, and shirts were haphazardly hung on hangers or lying on the floor. The only suit in a plastic dry cleaner's bag was the black suit at the back of the closet. He had worn it twice in the last sixteen months. He swore he would never wear it again.

Looking away from the suit, he randomly grabbed a suit, shirt, and tie. After getting dressed and tugging on his brown cowboy boots, that badly needed a polish, he stood in front of the dresser mirror to knot his tie.

The shirt and suit had changed nothing. The hollow-eyed, devastated man was still there. And Chance didn't know how long he could keep the man hidden. Last night had been a perfect example. One second, he'd been sitting there watching his brother and Delaney dance, and the next second, a certain Rascal Flatts song came on and an avalanche of memories and pain flooded him.

When someone had offered him a glass of spiked punch, he'd taken it. But one glass hadn't worked to douse the pain. It had taken much more to finally erase the memory of whirling a beautiful blonde with laughing blue eyes in his arms at his own wedding reception.

Erasing the memory had given him a new one.

A memory of mussed, multicolored hair. Sleepy whiskey-hazel eyes. A broken-heart tattoo covering the swell of one soft breast. Rosy nipples pressed against white cotton. And a tanned stomach studded with two glittering diamonds.

He squeezed his eyes shut and blocked out the memory before he headed for the door.

Since the garage was filled with boxes he'd yet to unpack, he parked his truck in the driveway. He could have walked to Holy Gospel Church. It was only a block away, but the Texas humidity was already thick and Chance's head still felt like an exposed wound.

On the drive to the church, he mentally went over the sermon he planned to give that morning. It was a standard sermon he'd gotten off the internet. He no longer had the inspiration to write his own. The church board *should* ask for his resignation. He shouldn't be a pastor. The only reason he had taken the job in Cursed was for Shane.

Ever since Chance had quit his pastoring job in Austin, Shane had been worried about him. He had found the job in Cursed and pulled the twin switch to get it for Chance. Since Chance didn't want his brother to worry—or to look like a jerk in front of Delaney—he had accepted it. Chance knew the minute he'd seen Shane and Delaney together that she was the girl for his brother.

He'd also known the minute he'd met Everly that she wasn't.

Shane had introduced them in college. Everly and Shane had been going to the University of Texas and Chance had been attending Dallas Christian College. It had been obvious from the first that Everly was a wild college girl who was more concerned with keg parties than studying. Since their father's life had been ruined by falling for the wrong girl, Chance had worried Shane might go down the same path.

He was still worried.

Which was why he couldn't leave Cursed until Everly was gone. Shane was all the family Chance had left. He refused to let a temptress ruin his brother's happiness. And there was no doubt Everly was a temptress.

An image of a diamond-studded belly button popped into his head, but he pushed it right back out as he pulled into Holy Gospel's parking lot.

The church was small but quaint. Made of Austin stone, it had a tall steeple that ran along the front of the main chapel and beautiful stained-glass windows that ran along either side. From what he'd heard, the church had been rebuilt in the 1950s and sat in the same spot as the original town church that had been built in the eighteen hundreds. The only thing remaining of the old church was the solid maple pulpit that Chance preached from every Sunday and the huge cross that hung on the wall behind the pulpit.

Inside the church was as hot and muggy as outside. Chance figured the air conditioner was on the fritz again. He had planned to buy a new one, but most of the church's coffers had been spent after tornados swept through Texas.

While there had only been limited damage to Cursed—the Malones' house and Mystic Malone's basement hair salon—there had been other people across the state who had lost their homes and businesses and needed money for food, clothing, and lodging until they could rebuild. Chance would just have to find another way to raise the money for the air conditioner.

"Good morning, Reverend Ransom."

Chance turned to see his receptionist coming down the hallway. Mrs. Moody was a retired schoolteacher who had volunteered to help out the previous pastor until he found a replacement. He never had. So Mrs. Moody was still the receptionist. And an efficient one. She was a tall, thin woman with a stern manner . . . and squeaky shoes.

"Good mornin', Mrs. Moody," he said loud enough to be heard over the squeak.

She stopped and fanned herself with the stack of Sunday programs she held in her hand. "It's stifling in here again. I'll ask Mr. Olson to take a look at the air conditioner—but little good it will do. The man doesn't know a screwdriver from a crescent wrench."

"He tries his best."

She snorted. "I don't know about that, but I guess he'll have to do. It isn't easy finding good help in a small town. After the way he was drinking and dancing last night, I'm sure he'll be late getting here this morning." She sent him a pointed look. "I'm surprised you're here so early."

He felt his face heat. "I apologize for my inappropriate behavior last night."

Her eyes widened. "Inappropriate? From what I could tell, all you were doing was having a little fun, Reverend. And if you were acting inappropriate, everyone else was too. I'll be surprised if anyone shows up for church today.

But be prepared for a full house in the next couple months. During the holidays, everyone wants to act like good Christians."

Chance didn't even want to think about the upcoming holidays. Last Thanksgiving and Christmas, every tradition, decoration, and carol had brought back painful memories.

"And speaking of Christmas," Mrs. Moody continued. "In the announcement today, you'll need to mention that the auditions for *Cowboy Scrooge* are coming up." She handed him a program. "I also put it in here, but few people read the program. Today, more than likely, they'll be using it as a fan. You might also mention that rehearsals start right after Thanksgiving and last until the performance the Saturday night before Christmas Eve."

Mrs. Moody had told him about the musical the church put on every year, so he nodded. "I'll be sure to announce it. Are you directing the play?" Mrs. Moody was not only the receptionist, but also the organist and the organizer of most church activities.

"No, I'm the Ghost of Christmas Past. The pastor of the church always directs the Christmas musical."

Chance stared at her. "Me?" The last thing he wanted to do was direct a Christmas play. It would be hard enough faking holiday cheer during church services. He certainly couldn't do it through a month of rehearsals. "I'm sorry, Mrs. Moody, but I'm not a play director. I wouldn't know where to start. I'm sure we can find someone to volunteer for the job."

She snorted. "Like you found someone to replace me and an experienced handyman to fix the air conditioner?"

It was a good point, but there had to be someone. "What about Miss Kitty? She seems to love being involved in everything." That was an understatement. Kitty Carson delivered the mail and all the town gossip. She prided herself on knowing everyone else's business ... and being in everyone's business.

"Kitty is playing the Ghost of Christmas Present and that woman loves the spotlight too much to give up a lead role to direct."

"How about Hester Malone or her granddaughter, Mystic?"

"Hester is the Ghost of Christmas Future. And Mystic does the hair, makeup, set design, and helps Hester with the costumes."

Chance was confused. "If we know what everyone's parts are, why do we need an audition?"

"We have to find a new Scrooge. Old Barney Sims was the best Scrooge you ever did see. His transformation from money-grubbing sinner to generous-hearted saint never failed to bring the house down. But sadly, Barney passed away in June. We also need to find a Tiny Wrangler Tim and Billy Bob Cratchit, but those parts aren't as crucial to the play. Without a Cowboy Scrooge, there'll be no musical."

Chance saw his way out and took it. "Then maybe we should skip the play this year. I think everyone will be sad to see someone else play Scrooge when it's always been Barney's part."

Mrs. Moody nodded. "Maybe you're right. Although we always use the ticket sales for charity and I was thinking this year charity could start at home and we could use it to get a new air conditioner."

A trickle of sweat ran down the back of Chance's neck, with it, any desire to cancel the musical. "I'll bring up the auditions this morning." Hopefully, while looking for a Scrooge, he could also find someone to direct.

But an hour later, when he stepped up to the pulpit, his prospects didn't look good. Mrs. Moody was right. The wedding reception had put a huge dent in the usual Sunday congregation. Those that were in attendance, looked as hungover as he felt. Since there was no hiding the elephant in the room, he decided to address it.

"Good morning. From the looks of things, we all enjoyed last night a little too much."

There was a round of chuckles and "amens" before an annoying voice rang out. "Looks like you more than most, Preach."

His gaze snapped to the back of the church.

Everly strutted down the aisle in sky-high heels and a lime-green dress that was completely inappropriate for church. As was her hair. She'd twisted the multicolored strands into some kind of messy bun that made her look like she was getting ready to step into a bubble bath.

What was she doing here?

As she sashayed to the very first row and sat

down, his mind was suddenly crowded with images. Images that had no business being in his head. Especially in church. And yet, there they were in vivid color. Mile-long, bronze legs tangled in light turquoise bedsheets. Rosy nipples muted beneath white cotton. A deep red heart tattoo with a black jagged crack through the center.

He pulled his gaze from Everly and blinked the images away. "Let's rise for the opening hymn."

Since he had never had a good singing voice, he usually mouthed the words and let the congregation carry the song. Except today no one seemed to be in a singing mood and all you could hear was Mrs. Moody playing the organ. And her organ-playing skills were mediocre at best. Chance had just decided to cut the hymn short when a clear soprano voice rang out.

He didn't know what surprised him more—Everly's amazing singing voice or the fact that she knew the hymn. She seemed to read his shock because a slight smirk tipped up one corner of her mouth and her eyes twinkled with amusement. Refusing to let her get the best of him, he stared back at her and started singing. The infuriating woman actually harmonized and made him sound good.

Which annoyed him even more.

If that was possible.

Everything about Everly grated on his nerves. She was too loud, too blunt, too . . . much. The rest of the service, she continued to irritate him with her perfect singing voice, and her loud

"Amen, Preach!" during his sermon, and her inappropriate dress and hair, and the smirk on her red-painted lips and the twinkle in her whiskey eyes. A smirk and twinkle that said she knew a secret that no one else knew. He figured that was why she had decided to attend church—to rub his nose in the fact that he'd passed out in her bed.

When the service was over, he always stood at the door and greeted people as they left the church. Everly was the last one in line.

"Hey, Preach. That's quite a singing voice you got there."

"What are you doing here? I thought you didn't want to be preached at."

She tipped her head. "Now is that any way to greet a person coming to your church for spiritual guidance? Or the woman who graciously offered you use of her bed last night?"

He glanced around to make sure everyone had left the church before he spoke. "Be honest, Everly. You didn't come here for spiritual guidance. Your spirit is the last thing you're worried about."

"Are you saying I'm carnal, Preach?"

Why the word would make his body flush with heat, he didn't know. Or maybe he just refused to know. "Why are you here, Everly?"

She sighed. "You really are no fun, Chance Ransom. But fine. You want me to get to the point of my church visit. I'll get to the point." The twinkle in her eyes faded. "No one tells me where I can live and where I can't. If I want to live in Cursed, Texas, I'll live in Cursed, Texas."

"Not if you're trying to take away my brother's happiness you won't."

"Like I told you before, that's not my plan."

"It doesn't have to be in your plan. Sometimes temptation is hard to resist."

She batted her eyelashes. "And now I'm tempting?"

"As tempting as a poisonous apple."

She laughed. "I think I like that analogy. Nothing like a poison apple to add a nice twist to a story."

"Shane and Delaney's story doesn't need a plot twist." He leaned closer. Close enough to catch the scent of something heady and womanly. He took a step back. "Leave, Everly. Not just for Shane's sake, but for your own. Nothing good comes from loving someone who can't love you back."

Everly stared at him for a long moment before she spoke. "And you would know that better than most, wouldn't you, Chance?" Her words struck like arrows straight to his heart and he struggled to catch his breath as she continued. "You're right. Nothing good comes from loving someone when they can't return that love. But while you've decided to hide from your pain and pretend that you're just fine and dandy, I've decided to face it head-on. I guess we'll have to see which way works the best." She paused. "And which one of us will be able to finally move on."

# Chapter Three

"WHAT ABOUT IF Ralph Potts played Cowboy Scrooge? He certainly looks the part." Mystic Malone sprayed a toxic amount of hairspray on Kitty Carson's bright red hair.

Everly, who was sitting on the couch in the lobby waiting her turn, thought Kitty would complain. Instead, she grabbed the can from Mystic and added another fog of spray before she waved it out of her face and spoke.

"I already thought about Potts for the part."

"I'm sure you did, Gossip Girl," Hester Malone said from her perch on a stool behind the appointment desk. As the town fortune-teller, the people of Cursed believed Hester could read your past, present, and future with just a glance. Everly didn't believe in psychic powers, but she understood why the townsfolk did. Hester had a piercing gaze and a spooky way of looking through a person. That gaze was focused on Kitty. "I've seen you chasing Potts around town in your mail truck."

Kitty swiveled in the salon chair to scowl at Hester. The two women had a strange relationship.

Everly wasn't sure if they were friends or enemies. They seemed to hang out a lot. Everly constantly saw Kitty's mail truck parked in front of the Malones' house and Hester and Kitty chatting on the front porch. But they also seemed to love goading each other.

"And you call me Gossip Girl, Witchy Woman," Kitty said. "I'll have you know that I never chase men while on duty. Only when I'm off duty." She scowled. "And it hasn't done me one speck of good. Either Potts can't take the hint or your prediction is wrong and he doesn't like me."

"He likes you. He's just shy with women. If you talk him into being Scrooge, maybe it will help him get over his shyness."

Kitty shook her head. "The man can't be Cowboy Scrooge. He can't carry a tune in a bucket. But maybe he could be Billy Bob Cratchit. Billy Bob only has a speaking part."

"Speaking of carrying a tune." Hester's piercing gaze landed on Everly. "I didn't realize you could sing so well, Everly."

"Me neither," Kitty said. "And how did you know those hymns? You don't seem like the type that grew up singing in church."

"What's that supposed to mean?" Hester asked. "I'm sure I don't look like the type to go to church either, but I do. Not all churchgoers have helmet hair and gossip."

Before the two women could get in an argument, Everly cut in. "You're right, Kitty. I'm not much of a churchgoing girl. I just stop by occasionally to give myself a slight chance of making it through those pearly gates." She went back to thumbing through the hairstyling magazine and sipping the coffee she'd picked up from the town restaurant, Good Eats. She would have loved one of Otis's homemade donuts to go with her coffee, but they were a popular item and were all gone by the time she got there. Obviously, the early worm got the donut and Everly had never been an early riser.

Kitty got up from the salon chair. "Well, we sure would love you to stop by church more often, Everly. In fact, with that voice of yours, you should try out for the church Christmas musical."

"Thanks, but I have horrible stage fright." It was a lie. Everly had no desire to be in a church musical.

"So does Hester. She throws up before every performance." Kitty glanced at Hester and grinned smugly. "Thought you were being sneaky about slipping off to the bathroom, didn't you? But nothin' that happens in this town goes unnoticed by these two peepers." She used two fingers to point to her eyes. "They see all. And they saw something really interesting Sunday morning."

Hester sighed. "Here we go again."

"Now don't act like you don't enjoy a little juicy gossip, Hester. And this is some juicy gossip. I was coming back from checking on the post office after the wind set off the security alarm when I saw Reverend Ransom slipping into the parsonage looking like he had been rode hard and put away wet."

Everly had to spit her coffee back into the take-out cup to keep from choking on it.

"And so?" Hester said. "Maybe he'd gone out for his morning run. He runs past this house almost every morning at the crack of dawn." So that was where he got his hot body.

Kitty sent Hester a smug look. "In the same clothes he wore the night before?"

Hester's eyes widened. "He had on what he wore to the wedding reception?"

"The exact same thing, and his shirt and pants looked like they had been wadded up overnight . . . on a bedroom floor."

"Now don't be starting rumors," Hester said. "They could've been wadded up on his bedroom floor. The preacher did overdrink the other night."

"So why was he up so early? And even if he did get up early to get a donut at Good Eats, why would he wear his wrinkled clothes? I'm tellin' you that our preacher hooked up with someone at the reception. That was a walk of shame if ever I saw one."

The snort of laughter that came out of Everly's mouth had everyone turning to her.

"Sorry," she said. "But I just have a hard time picturing our uptight pastor taking the walk of shame." She leaned closer to Kitty and spoke in a low voice. "Who do you think it is, Miss Kitty? Who do you think would lead our sweet little ol' preacher astray?"

"I don't have a clue. But I plan to find out.

There were only so many single women at the weddin'."

Everly widened her eyes dramatically. "Unless, of course, it was a married woman."

Kitty pressed a hand to her chest. "Lord have mercy. Let's hope that's not the case. That would be a cryin' shame, I tell you. Just a cryin' shame. The pastor falling in love with a single woman is one thing, but him just enjoying carnal sex is another."

"I don't think we should be making assumptions." Mystic entered the conversation. "It's not any of our business what Chance does in his private life."

"Of course it's our business." Kitty stared at Mystic in shock. "We spent a long time looking for someone to take over after Reverend Floyd retired. If we lose Reverend Ransom, who knows how long we'll have to go without a pastor. Chance was the only one who applied."

Chance hadn't applied. Shane had done the twin switch and applied for him. Everly wasn't so sure Chance had even wanted the job. She still wasn't sure. Being a lost soul, she recognized one when she saw one. Chance was as lost as she was. But while she was working to find her way, it looked like he'd completely given up hope. As much as his self-righteousness annoyed her, she kind of felt sorry for him.

Which was why she hadn't been exactly truthful about what had happened the night of Mystic and Buck's wedding. They hadn't had sex, but they had done something they had no business doing.

"I agree with Kitty," Hester said. "We can't let Chance leave Cursed. He needs us as much as we need him."

"Have you seen something, Hester?" Kitty asked.

"You know I don't talk about what I've seen with anyone but who it concerns. But it doesn't take sight to know Chance needs love and support right now after losing his wife and his beloved grandmother all in one year."

Kitty shook her head, sadly. "Just a cryin' shame, I tell you. Just a cryin' shame. And you're right, Hester. We need to help him get over his grief. The best way to help a man get over the loss of a woman is to find him a new one. We just need to make sure the woman he gets with isn't a shameless hussy."

Being the shameless hussy, Everly couldn't help playing along. "You are so right, Miss Kitty. We can't have our new preacher marrying anyone but a sweet, virginal country gal. And no sweet, virginal country gal would lure the preacher into her bed for the night."

Kitty's eyes narrowed in thought. "That's a good point. We need to find that man a good woman to wed before he's tempted by the devil again." She turned to Mystic. "We'll need your help, Mystic."

According to gossip, Mystic was as psychic as her grandmother. But while Hester predicted the future, Mystic read love auras. Supposedly, she could tell if someone was in love by the golden haze encircling their heads. Everly didn't believe for a second Mystic had that kind of power. And even if she did, there was no way in hell Chance had a golden aura. He was still too emotionally strung out. And if anyone knew what emotionally strung out looked like, it was Everly.

She wasn't ready to fall in love again either, and she didn't know if she ever would be.

Mystic pulled a purple cape out of the drawer at her station and shook it out. "Sorry, but I'm not getting involved in any matchmaking scheme. I think we need to leave Chance alone and let him deal with his grief as he sees fit. Come on over, Everly. I'm ready for you."

When Everly got up and headed for the salon chair, Kitty grabbed her mailbag by the door. "I better get back to work. Tally me up, Witchy Woman. Then you can follow me out to the truck. I got a package for you. From the size and weight, I think it might be that crystal ball you ordered."

Once Kitty had paid and the two women left, Everly glanced at Mystic in the mirror. "A crystal ball?"

Mystic nodded. "Her old one disappeared in the tornado."

"And just where do you get crystal balls?"

"Amazon."

Everly laughed. "Of course."

Mystic picked up a brush and ran it through Everly's hair. "So what are we doing today?"

Everly looked at her reflection. She had thought

having her hair color melted in a range of platinum-blond to jet-black had been cool. But the appeal had worn off. Now when she looked in the mirror she felt like the rainbow-haired doll her daddy had gotten her for Christmas one year. Plastic and fake. And plastic and fake were two things Everly never wanted to be.

"I think I'll go with my natural dark brown."

She didn't completely trust a small-town stylist, but it turned out her fears were ungrounded. Mystic was an experienced hairstylist who seemed to know exactly what she was doing. Or at least, that's what Everly thought until she looked in the mirror at the finished product. The hair that fell in a smooth, slick fall around her face and shoulders wasn't dark brown. It was a rich auburn with magenta and red wine highlights that gleamed in the salon lights like flames.

It might not be what she asked for, but it looked good. Damn good.

She studied her reflection in the mirror. "I'd call this more vampire slut-red than natural dark brown."

Mystic turned away and started straightening her station. "Sorry. I must've gotten the dye numbers confused."

Everly could believe she'd gotten one color wrong. But there was no way she'd gotten the base color and highlights wrong. It didn't take a genius to figure out why Mystic was lying.

"You thought I wanted you to make my hair dark like Delaney Kingman's, didn't you?" Everly said. "Which is why you made sure mine looks nothing like hers."

Mystic hesitated before she turned to Everly. "I know you still love Shane."

"I guess you read my love aura."

"It's hard not to read. Like I told you before, I don't want you making trouble for Delaney."

Everly couldn't fault Mystic for wanting to watch out for her friend. Just like she couldn't fault Chance for watching out for his brother.

She held up her hands. "Okay, so I still love Shane. Sue me. But I'm not trying to break up his and Delaney's marriage."

"Then why did you take the job at Nasty's?"

She had never felt like she had to explain her actions to anyone. Which was why she hadn't explained them to Chance. But since Mystic was the only hairstylist in town and Everly didn't want to end up bald, she figured it was time for the truth.

"Delaney talked me into it."

Mystic stared at her. "Delaney? Why would she do that?"

"Because she isn't the type of woman who hides from things. That's how she got me to move here. She thinks the only way for me to get over Shane is to witness for myself how ecstatically happy he is. And she's right. Seeing him this happy has made me realize that he made the right choice. He didn't need some indecisive woman who dyes her hair a different color every month, had three different majors in college, and has had six different jobs in the last four years. He needed a strong country gal who knows what she wants and can give him the security he didn't have growing up."

Mystic studied her. "It sounds like your brain gets it, but what about your heart?"

Obviously, Mystic *could* read love auras.

Everly sighed. "Hearts have a little longer learning curves. But it will get there. And I'm not staying in Cursed, Mystic. I plan to leave as soon as Gretchen delivers her baby and is ready to come back to work."

Mystic's shoulders relaxed and she sighed. "I'm sorry. I told Hester and Kitty they didn't have any business butting their noses into Chance's business, but then I butted my nose into yours. You can't help who you fall in love with. I should know that better than most."

"Don't tell me you didn't want to fall in love with Buck."

"Not when we were younger. I didn't see a love aura around him and thought he would never return my love."

"So I guess your psychic powers aren't always right."

Mystic shook her head. "Which is why I've stopped giving love advice and now strictly do hair." She studied Everly's hair and frowned. "I'm sorry about yours. If you have the time, I'll be happy to turn you into a brunette."

"Like hell, you will." Everly looked back at the mirror. "I think red might be my color."

Mystic looked relieved as she unsnapped the cape. "That's good because I would've had to cancel my next appointment and Buck would've thought I did it for him. We got into a big fight about me cutting men's hair."

Everly got up from the chair. "I take it you won."

"Of course. You give a Kingman an inch and they'll take a mile. I don't want Buck thinking he can tell me what to do in my own—"

The bell over the door jangled and cut her off. Everly turned to see Chance stepping into the salon. He wore a sky-blue western shirt, faded jeans, and the same brown cowboy boots and hat he'd worn to the reception. The hat was pulled low on his forehead, but she didn't have to see his eyes to know the second he noticed her.

He froze in the doorway.

"Hey, Chance!" Mystic said. "Come on in and have a seat on the couch. I just need to grab a broom from the back and clean up my station and I'll be right with you."

Once Mystic was gone, Everly turned to Chance and placed a hand on her hip. "So? What do you think of my new do, Preach?" When he didn't answer, she prodded. "What? Do my flaming locks leave you speechless?"

He took off his hat and placed it on the coatrack. "Everything you do leaves me speechless."

"Now stop flirting, you rascal, or you'll turn my head. And we wouldn't want Miss Kitty finding out I was the shameless hussy who made you do the walk of shame."

He turned back to her. "What are you talking about? What's a walk of shame?"

She shook her head. "You really need to get out more. It's what people do when they sneak out the morning after a regrettable night of wild sex. I guess Kitty saw you going into your house Sunday morning looking like a cat that had been dragged behind Buck's monster truck."

Chance's eyes widened. He glanced at the doorway to the back room before stepping closer. "Miss Kitty saw me?"

Everly tried to keep her mind on the question and not on the scent that tickled her nose when he moved closer. It was the same scent he'd left on her sheets. Something musky and intriguing and not at all belonging to a boring preacher. He had a little smudge of toothpaste in the corner of his stern lips.

Lips she had tasted.

Why she had kissed him the other night, she still didn't know. Maybe the same reason she wanted to kiss him now. She had never been able to resist men who were all wrong for her. Chance was all wrong. He was a preacher. An ex-lover's brother. A lost soul who had no desire to be found.

*Snap out of it, Everly!*

She pulled her gaze from his mouth and tried to refocus on the question he'd just asked. "Apparently, nothing escapes Kitty's peepers."

He sighed and ran a hand through his hair. She had never liked his short, slicked-back pastor hair, but she liked this finger-tousled hair. She hoped he didn't have Mystic cut too much off. "What am I going to do?" he asked. "You know Kitty is going to corner me first chance she gets."

"Oh, you can count on it. So, like the Grinch, I'd be thinking of a lie and thinking it up quick."

He sent her an annoyed look. "You want me to lie?"

"You already cuss, fight, and drink. A little lie isn't going to send you to hell any faster."

"Gee, thanks for making me feel like the worst preacher ever."

She smiled. "You're welcome. And while I'm pointing out all your flaws, you have a little toothpaste right here." She took his chin in the crook of her finger and brushed her thumb over the corner of his mouth.

It was just a simple touch. There was nothing sexual about it. But if that was true, then why did she suddenly feel like she'd just experienced her first menopausal hot flash? And why had she yet to remove her hand from his chin? Or her thumb from the plump swell of his bottom lip?

And why hadn't he pulled away?

He just stood staring back at her as if her touch had turned him into stone. Just not solid stone. His eyes held the same steamy warmth that was bubbling deep inside of her. But the steamy look only lasted for a second before his eyes narrowed.

"You lied."

## Chapter Four

"ARE YOU FEELING all right, Reverend?"

Chance swiveled his desk chair around from the window he'd been staring out of to find Mrs. Moody standing in the doorway of his office. "I'm fine, Mrs. Moody. Why do you ask?"

"You seemed a little upset all day. I hope you're not worried about the musical auditions tonight."

He hadn't even remembered the auditions. His mind was preoccupied with something else entirely. Like the memories that had flooded back when Everly had touched him.

She'd lied. Something *had* happened between them the night of the reception. Something his brain had worked hard to repress. He wished it had continued to repress it. He did not want to deal with the mistake he'd made—the sin he'd committed.

"Reverend?"

He returned his attention to Mrs. Moody, realizing she was still waiting for his reply. "No, I'm not concerned about the auditions." To be honest, he was hoping they wouldn't find a Scrooge so they could cancel the show. He would figure out another way to get money for the air conditioner.

Mrs. Moody nodded. "Well, I guess I'll be heading home then."

"Thank you, Mrs. Moody. Have a good evening."

She started to leave, but then stopped and turned back to him. "I'm not one to gossip. Or pay too much attention to other people's gossip." After finding out Kitty had seen him sneaking back into his house, Chance figured he knew where this was going. Her next words confirmed it. "I just want to say that if you have a girlfriend that's nobody's business but yours."

"Well, thank you for your support, Mrs. Moody, but I don't have a girlfriend."

Her eyes turned sad. "Oh. I was hoping that maybe . . ." She let the sentence drift off before she continued. "It's just that I know what you're going through. After Jeffrey passed, I was heartbroken. I thought I would never be happy again. But after a time, I did find happiness. And you will too. You just need to have faith."

Faith.

Ever since Lori passed, Chance had struggled with his faith. His lack of faith was why he'd quit the church in Austin and why he shouldn't have accepted the job here in Cursed. But besides wanting to keep Shane from worrying about him, there was something about the small town that had struck a spark of hope in Chance. The town's ancestors had endured every natural disaster known to man—tornados, floods, drought, and pestilence. Through it all, the townsfolk had kept their faith and built a little country church to worship in. If they could do it, Chance had hoped that maybe he could too. But that hope was dying with each passing day.

As if reading his thoughts, Mrs. Moody walked over in her squeaky shoes and placed a hand on his shoulder. "Believe me, I know it's hard. All you can do is keep getting up every day and trying your best."

After she left, Chance sat there for a long moment thinking about her words. He had been getting up every morning, even the mornings he didn't want to. But he had to admit that he hadn't been trying his best. He'd only been sleepwalking through life. Going through the motions without much thought or effort.

Which was how he'd ended up having sex with Everly.

Since realizing more had happened the other night than Everly had confessed, he'd tried to avoid the *sex* word. But he couldn't avoid it any longer. While the memories of that night were foggy, they weren't foggy enough. He remembered kissing Everly. Touching her. And as much as he would like to continue to ignore what happened, he couldn't. He might have lost his faith, but he hadn't lost his sense of responsibility.

He glanced at the clock on the bookshelf. He had two hours before auditions started. That should give him plenty of time.

Thankfully, Nasty Jack's wasn't busy on

Thursdays, especially that early in the evening. When Chance walked in the door, there were only a couple of people playing pool in the back and one cowboy sitting at the bar . . . flirting with Everly.

Chance sat down at the other end of the bar and waited for her to notice him. She was unloading the dishwasher as she talked with the cowboy. She wore a tight pair of skinny jeans and a Nasty Jack's T-shirt that she'd knotted at her waist so that every time she reached up to place the glasses she removed from the dishwasher on a shelf, her stomach showed.

And the belly button diamonds.

An image of him brushing his tongue over the diamonds popped into his head. He didn't know if it was a memory or just a fantasy. Either way, he pushed it right back out and listened in on Everly and the cowboy's conversation.

"I think you are full of crap, Hayden," she said. "You did not beat Jesse Wright at bronc riding."

"I sure as hell did." Hayden stood and pulled up his T-shirt to reveal a huge silver rodeo belt buckle.

Everly stopped unloading the dishwasher and leaned over the bar for a closer look. "Well, I'll be damned. Can I touch it?"

A stab of annoyance hit Chance. Before she could reach over the bar, he called her name. Maybe a little louder than necessary.

"Everly!"

The cowboy glanced over, but Everly didn't even look in his direction. Which made him realize she had known he was sitting there the entire time.

She ran a finger over the embossed silver buckle. "I'm sure this has gotten you in more women's beds than you can count."

Chance's jaw tightened. "Everly."

She didn't look at him, but Hayden did. "Uhh . . . Everly. I think the preacher is trying to get your attention."

She straightened and turned to Chance. "Oh, hey, Preach. What brings you into Nasty's? I don't have any wedding punch, but I could fix you an Orgasm. The drink, of course. Not the real thing."

"I didn't come here for a drink," he said. "I came to talk."

"Sorry, but I'm working." She went back to unloading the dishwasher.

"Everly." When she glanced up, he added. "Please."

She sighed. "I'll be right back, Hayden." She moved down the bar and stopped in front of Chance. "Okay, so I lied. I thought it would be easier for you to forgive yourself if you didn't know exactly what sins you'd committed. And I still think it's better if you don't. There's no reason to go through every sordid detail. In fact, I'd just as soon forget it myself."

He wished it were that easy. But the details of their night together kept popping into his head at the most inopportune times. Like now, when an image of sliding her full bottom lip between his teeth flashed through his head. He pulled his gaze from her mouth.

"I'm not here to go through every detail." He didn't need or want any more fodder for his brain. "I'm here to make sure we used something."

Her eyebrows lifted. "Like sex toys?"

He rolled his eyes. "No. Like contraception."

"Ahh, so you're worried about a little Chance sprouting. Or are you more worried about catching some nasty disease? Well, let me put your mind at ease, Preach. I'm on birth control and disease free. Not that it matters because we didn't have sex. We only shared a couple kisses."

"And you expect me to believe you when you lied before?"

"I'm not lying this time. If you brought your Bible with you, I'd be happy to swear on it."

He studied her for a long moment. She didn't look away. The tension he'd been feeling released and he gave a heavy sigh.

She laughed. "Way to stroke a woman's ego, Preach. Now if you'll excuse me, I need to get back to work."

He would have let her go if something hadn't struck him as odd. "You said you were drunk Saturday night. But you weren't too drunk to close up the bar."

"I have a higher tolerance of alcohol than you do."

"Then you knew what you were doing."

She shrugged. "Okay. So I was the one who kissed you. Is that what you needed to hear?"

He should have let it go. But for some reason, he didn't. "Why? Why did you kiss me?" Her hesitation was answer enough. "It was because I look like Shane, wasn't it?"

A flare of hurt entered her eyes. "Maybe you're right, Preach. But I wasn't the only one pretending I was in bed with someone else. If memory serves, Shane wasn't the name that brought an end to our make-out session. It was Lor—"

He cut in. "Stop. I don't need to hear any more."

"Oh, so now you don't want to talk. Well, you waltzed in here wanting to know the truth so let's get to the truth. I'm a pathetic lovesick fool, but at least I can say Shane's name. You have to be totally drunk off your ass before you can bring yourself to say—"

"Don't."

Everly stared at him as if he'd grown horns. "You can't even hear her name, can you?"

"I have to go. I have auditions at the church." He started to get up, but she reached over the bar and grabbed his arm. Just like at Mystic's salon, Everly's touch made him . . . feel.

He didn't want to feel.

"Come on, Preach, say it. It's not a difficult name. Just four little letters and two syllables. Lor—"

He jerked away from her and headed out the door. Once in his truck, his hands were shaking so badly he couldn't even push the ignition button. He closed his eyes and tried to calm his nerves with deep breaths. The sound of the truck door opening had his eyelids lifting. Everly slid into the passenger seat.

"I don't want to talk anymore," he said.

"I didn't come out here to talk. I just wanted to make sure you were okay. But that was stupid. You're about as far from okay as a person can get." She hesitated. "Look, I'm sorry. I had no business making you say her name—even though I think it would do you good to get it out. But that's not any of my business. And just to be clear, I didn't just kiss you because you look like Shane. I have a thing for men who are all wrong for me and alcohol exacerbates the problem. Thankfully, calling me by another woman's name brought me back to my senses. If you hadn't, I'm sure we would've done the nasty." Her gaze lowered to his mouth. "You are one damn good kisser, Preach. That sweepy thing you do with your tongue almost made me or—" She cut off. "Sorry. Too much information."

"Way too much." Her words had made his entire body flush with heat.

She laughed. "We make quite a pair, don't we? You say too little and I say too much."

"I wouldn't call us a pair. We're more like vinegar and oil."

"I guess I'm the vinegar in that analogy. I hate to break this to you, but vinegar and oil *are* a pair. They go perfect on a salad. You just have to shake them up."

An image of their tongues brushing together flashed into his mind, but he quickly blinked it away. "We're not a pair, Everly."

"Don't get your panties in a bunch, Preach. I don't want to pair up with you either. Although you're going to be paired up soon enough if Kitty has her way."

"So I heard." He sighed and took off his cowboy hat. He didn't realize until he ran his hand through his hair that he'd stopped shaking.

"You didn't get a haircut."

He glanced over. "What?"

"You didn't cut your hair."

"Oh. No, I was . . ."

"Too freaked out about having sex with the town hussy."

"You're not the town hussy. I'm just as much to blame for what happened. In fact, it was all my fault."

"All your fault? Maybe Kitty's right. You need a wife to keep you from taking yourself too serious."

"I'm not getting married again. I intend to make that clear to Kitty Carson. She doesn't know what I need and neither do you. Just because you know Shane, doesn't mean you know me."

She laughed. "Now that's funny. Being friends with Shane is exactly why I do know you. I've had to listen to story after story about you—from the time you and Shane were snot-nosed kids to the time you were arrogant college boys. I know about the chemistry set you begged Santa for and how when you got it, you ended up burning your lungs with some vile-smelling liquid you concocted and had to go to the emergency room. I know about the time you and Shane snuck out and tried to steal your grandma's old Plymouth and you convinced Shane you were the better driver and ran into the neighbor's mailbox. I know you felt the calling to become a preacher your senior year of high school. And how you first met . . . The One Who Shall Not Be Named right after college and fell head over holy boots in love."

He stared at her. "Shane told you all that?"

She nodded. "In case you didn't realize it, your brother loves the shit out of you. We couldn't have one conversation without him bragging about you."

"I wouldn't call me burning my lungs or running over a mailbox something to brag about."

"Of course, they are. They prove that Reverend Ransom is human."

"I think I've more than proved that since coming to Cursed."

She smiled. She had one of those smiles that transformed her face. It added warmth to her stunning features and made her seem much more approachable. As did her hair. The new color reminded him of a blazing campfire on a starry night. He wanted to put his hands to the silky strands to see if they gave off heat.

"I gotta tell you, Preach," she said. "I like the sinning human much better than I like the holier-than-thou preacher."

"I'm not holier-than-thou."

"You have been to me."

He couldn't deny it. He *had* been a judgmental jerk to Everly ever since he'd first met her. He'd judged her revealing clothing and blunt outspokenness. He had worried she would pull his brother away from his studies. After college, he had worried she'd pull Shane away from his career goals. She'd done neither. Instead, she had pushed Shane to study hard and had supported his dream of starting his own software development company.

She loved Shane.

But never in a destructive kind of way.

"I'm sorry," he said.

"For what? Being a holier-than-thou? Or for the fooling-around part?"

"For both."

"Now don't go back to beating yourself up, Preach. Pastors make mistakes just like anyone else. And you've had one hell of a year. So I think God will give you a Get-Out-Of-Hell-Free card this one time."

"A Get-Out-Of-Hell-Free card?" He couldn't help but laugh.

Everly stared at him. "Did I just make you laugh?"

He sobered. "No."

She tipped her head, causing her hair to spill over her shoulder in a satiny curtain of stunning red. "Yes, I did. Are we becoming friends, Preach?"

"Not likely. Now get out of my truck. I have to find a Scrooge."

"Have you tried looking in the mirror?"

He pointed a finger. "Out!"

She stuck her tongue at him before she opened the door and hopped out. He waited until she was safely inside the bar before he headed back to the parsonage.

On the way, he said one word.

"Lori."

Surprisingly, it didn't hurt as much as he thought it would.

## Chapter Five

EVERLY WAS STILL smiling when she stepped back into Nasty Jack's. Her smile faded when she saw Hayden coming out of the kitchen with two plates of pie. She hurried over to take them from him.

"Hey, you just had to keep an eye on the cash register. You didn't have to serve pie."

"It's not a big deal. I worked in a diner when I was first rodeoing to make ends meet. I mostly cooked, but, occasionally, when a waitress called in sick, I had to wait tables too."

Everly stared at him. "You know how to cook?"

"I'm passable."

She was stunned. She had thought Hayden West only knew rodeoing and cowboying. He had shown up in Cursed around the same time as she had taken on managing the bar. He'd given up the rodeo and was now working at the Kingman Ranch. He'd become a regular at Nasty Jack's. On slow nights, Everly had gotten to know him pretty well. He had the rodeo-cowboy cock and swagger, but was a genuine, hardworking man who Everly trusted enough to leave in charge of watching the cash register.

The fact he had worked in a diner as a cook was an intriguing piece of information. She and Wolfe had been searching for a cook to take over for Gretchen during her maternity leave for a few months now with no luck. Maybe their luck had changed.

After serving the pie to the truckers playing pool, she returned to the bar. "When you say passable, are you talking passably good or passably there's a possibility that people could get food poisoning?"

He laughed. "It's hard to judge your own cooking, but I'd say it was passably good."

Everly rested her arms on the bar and smiled. "How would you like a job, good-lookin' rodeo man?" It wasn't an understatement. Hayden was one good-looking cowboy. Just not one she was interested in. He was too nice and available. She really was screwed up.

"I have a job at the Kingman Ranch," he said.

"I know, but I'm sure we could work something out where you could swap off working here and at the ranch. You'd only have to work Monday through Thursday. Otis and Thelma Davenport, who own the Good Eats Restaurant, help out on the weekends. And it would just be for a few months. Just until Gretchen Kingman has her baby—and possibly a couple months after that. From what I've heard, most new mommies and daddies like to stay home and stare at the miracle they created."

Hayden's eyebrows lifted. "I'm guessing by your tone you're not interested in motherhood."

"I don't know if I'm mother material."

"I don't think any women are born to be mothers. I think it's a choice you make."

"For now, I'm making the choice not to be one. Now about that job, do you want to help me out or not?"

"I would, but I might not be staying long in Cursed."

"You got somewhere else to be?"

He hesitated. "Not really."

"Then why not be a hero and help out a woman whose feet are swelling like cantaloupes because she spends too much time on them. Have you met Gretchen? She's just about the sweetest woman you'd ever want to meet. You want her to have cantaloupe feet?"

Hayden held up his hands. "Fine. I'll help out."

She slugged him in the arm. "Thanks, rodeo man. I owe you."

"I'd ask you on a date again, but my ego can't take another rejection."

She laughed as she picked up a towel and started polishing the bar. "Go sell that malarkey to someone else. Me turning you down hasn't hurt your inflated ego one bit."

Hayden placed a hand over his heart. "It most certainly has. Your rejection has wounded me for life. Especially now that I know you've thrown me over for a preacher."

She stopped polishing and turned to him. "What?"

Hayden grinned. "Don't try to deny it. If you didn't have a thing for Reverend Ransom, then why were you ignoring him so intently when he first stepped into the bar? And why did you race after him?"

"I didn't race after him." When Hayden quirked a brow, she sighed. "Okay, so maybe I did race after him, but it wasn't because I have a thing for him. It was because I opened my big mouth and said something I shouldn't have said."

"And you're trying to tell me you've never done that before? Because I gotta tell you, Everly, I've witnessed you saying things you probably shouldn't say to a lot of folks. You never seem to care about hurting their feelings."

"Chance is in a more sensitive place right now than most people."

Hayden squinted his eyes and studied her for a moment. "Okay. Have it your way. You don't have a thing for the preacher."

"Not at all. Now why don't you head back to the kitchen and whip us up some dinner? If you think I'm interested in Chance, I'm not sure I should trust your opinion of your cooking without tasting it first."

It turned out Hayden's opinion of his cooking was too humble. The sliders and wings he made for her were juicy and cooked to perfection and the French fries crispy and delicious. When she woke up the following morning, she couldn't wait to head out to the Kingman Ranch to give Wolfe and Gretchen the good news.

Everly hadn't been to the ranch often. In

fact, she'd only been there once for Shane and Delaney's wedding. It had been one of the hardest days of her life. She'd been so busy trying to smile and act like her heart wasn't breaking that she'd barely paid attention to her surroundings.

Of course, it was hard not to notice the house the Kingmans lived in.

Referred to as Buckinghorse Palace, the stone mansion with its tall turrets looked like a fairytale castle right out of the pages of a children's storybook. Next to the castle was an English garden where the wedding had been held. Everly remembered flowers and trees, but she didn't remember the quaint English cottage or the stone pathway or the profusion of color everywhere. Even this late in the year, flowers were blooming in fall shades of golds and oranges and reds.

As she stepped out of her car, she stopped for a moment to enjoy the beauty.

That's when she saw Shane. He was striding down the path of the garden. The morning sun gilded his hair—hair that always looked like it needed a good trim. When he saw her, his face lit up. He loved her. She had always known he loved her.

Just not enough.

"Ev!" He tried to open the garden gate, but his hands seemed to be filled with . . . kittens?

She hurried over and opened the gate for him, but kept a distance from the wiggling fur balls in his arms. "Let me guess, you've now added stray cats to your refuge for abused and neglected ranch animals."

"No. The barn cat had a litter. Del wanted to keep them all, but I talked her into just keeping two for our new refuge barn. I'm taking these three into town to see if I can find good homes for them." He shot her a glance and his eyebrows lifted beneath the brim of his cowboy hat.

She shook her head. "Don't look at me. You know I'm not an animal person. I'm too self-centered to take care of anything that's not me."

"I think you try to convince everyone that you aren't an animal person, but if that's the case, why are all your favorite movies about them—*Turner & Hooch, Babe, The Lion King*?"

"A person can like to watch animals, but just not want to get up close and personal with them. Believe me, I don't have an underlying desire to be Doctor Dolittle like you and Delaney obviously do."

"Fine. But could you grab the one who is using my chest as a scratching post?"

Everly sighed and carefully detached the tiger-striped kitten from Shane's chest. It was a soft, tiny little thing and she instantly worried she was going to hurt it. She'd never had animals as a kid. Her parents didn't want the hair or mess.

"Don't hold it out like that," Shane instructed. "Hold it close."

She hesitated before tucking the wiggling kitten against her chest. Surprisingly, it stopped wiggling and settled in like a fuzzy lump of warmth.

"Hey, Everly!" Wolfe came around the side of the house. "What are you doing here so early? I thought you slept in."

"I normally do. But I have some good news that couldn't wait. I found a cook."

"You're kidding?"

"Nope. And he was right under our noses. Hayden West."

Wolfe looked taken back. "Hayden? He can cook?"

She stroked the kitten's soft fur. "I guess he used to work in a diner. The only problem is that it might interfere with his ranch work here. Which is what I came to talk to you about."

"And here I thought you came to visit me," Shane said with a teasing smile. For some strange reason, she found herself comparing it to his brother's.

They had the same features so she thought their smiles would be the same. But they were completely different. Shane's smiles were wide and quick. He flashed most of his teeth all at once. Chance's smiles were much slower. They started with a twitch at the corner of his mouth, then a slight parting of his lips, and finally a full-fledged reveal of his pearly whites. Sort of like a sunrise peeking over the horizon. You had to wait for its full beauty.

"I'm sure we can work out Hayden's schedule," Wolfe said, pulling Everly from her strange train of thought. "Winter is always slower on the ranch. So we won't need Hayden here as much. He'll have plenty of time to take over for Gretchen."

"He can't completely take over for her," Everly said. "She still needs to make her pies or we'll have a town mutiny on our hands."

Wolfe laughed. "I couldn't get her to stop baking pies if I tried. The woman is in the kitchen right now creating different holiday pies to put on the menu. But I know she'll be thrilled to not have to go to the bar every night." He wrapped an arm around Everly and pulled her in for a side hug so he wouldn't squash the kitten.

After he'd started the bar fight over Shane breaking Delaney's heart, Everly had thought Wolfe was a tough alpha guy. But working at the bar with him for the last month had made her realize he was as big of a pussycat as the kitten sleeping in her arms.

"Thank you, Everly," he said. "Not just for finding someone to help Gretchen in the kitchen, but also for moving to Cursed and helping me with the bar. I don't know how I managed without you."

She drew back. "Now hold up there, Wolfe Kingman. I haven't moved to Cursed. I'm just helping out until Gretchen has her baby."

"I know." He winked. "But just so you know, I'm going to do everything in my power to get you to stay."

"It won't work," Shane said. "Ev is a city girl through and through."

Wolfe punched him in the arm, and from Shane's cringe, it hurt. "So were you, but now you're more of a country boy than I am. Now I'm going to go tell Gretchen the good news."

When Wolfe was gone, Everly handed the kitten back to Shane. "Take this fur ball. I need to go. I have numerous beer and liquor orders coming in today. Mystic and Buck's wedding reception cleaned us out."

"I don't know how. Most folks drank the punch. Did you spike it?"

"No. I'm not sure who did. But whoever it was had a heavy hand."

"You can say that again. It knocked me for a loop." He paused. "And Chance." He tried to stop the tiger-striped kitten from climbing over his shoulder. Scared it was going to fall, Everly pulled it back into her arms as Shane continued. "Did you happen to hear the gossip going around about my brother?"

"You mean Kitty seeing him sneak into his house early Sunday morning?"

Shane nodded. "It's ridiculous. Chance is too moral to spend the night with some woman. Although I wish he would. Maybe it would help him get over Lori."

"I doubt sex with another woman will get him over Lori." In fact, Everly didn't just doubt it. She knew it. He couldn't even hear the woman's name. And while pathetic, it was also endearing. What would it feel like to be loved like that?

"You're right. I just wish I knew what would."

"Chance just needs time. Time is supposed to heal all wounds."

Shane's eyes turned sad. "Has it healed yours, Ev?"

Normally, she made some joke to avoid talking about a subject she didn't want to talk about. But this time, she didn't. This time, she answered truthfully.

"Not completely, but I'm getting there. And in case you think that means I'm still pining away for you, I'm not. Yeah, my ego still feels bruised that I couldn't make you as happy as Delaney has. But I figure, one day, I'll find someone I can. I expect him to be totally and completely infatuated with me like you are with Del."

Shane smiled. "I don't think you'll have any trouble finding him."

"Of course I won't. I'm awesome. Now take this ball of fur so—"

Before she could hand the kitten back, the garage door opened and Delaney's truck backed out. Everly felt awkward about being caught talking to Shane. But Delaney didn't act the least bit jealous when she rolled down the window and peeked her head out.

"Hey, Ev! Nice hair. You look like that Disney mermaid."

Shane glanced back at her. "That's what's different. You changed your hair color."

"Way to be observant, honey buns," Delaney said. "Now come on. We need to go. Stetson just called and Lily's water broke while she was reading one of her books at the elementary school. They're on their way to the hospital now."

Shane handed off the other two kittens to Everly. "Take them into town and see if anyone wants them."

"Oh, no, Shane Ransom." She juggled the cats in her arms. "Don't you dare leave me with—"

But Shane was already in the truck with Delaney who was grinning like a fool. "Don't look so scared, Ev. I'm sure you'll have no trouble finding the cuties homes. People love kittens, especially around the holidays." She winked. "Or maybe Ariel will decide to keep Flounder, Scuttle, and Sebastian herself." She laughed at her joke before she took off down the road.

Leaving Everly to deal with three wiggling fur balls.

## Chapter Six

"CANCEL THE CHRISTMAS musical?"

Hester Malone looked at Chance as if he'd just told her that he was going to strangle a puppy. And the two other judges, Kitty Carson and Mrs. Moody, were looking at him the same way. He had thought the three women were hard to deal with separately. Together, they were a force to be reckoned with.

"We can't cancel the musical," Kitty continued. "Haven't you ever heard the saying 'the show must go on'? Neither sleet, nor hail, nor dark of night can keep me from delivering the mail. And the little ol' problem of finding a Cowboy Scrooge can't stop the show either."

"Kitty is right." Mrs. Moody got up from the piano and came down the steps to the pew Chance, Hester, and Kitty sat in. She had accompanied the people trying out for different parts. Which might have contributed to the off-key singing Chance had had to suffer through all evening. "You can't cancel the musical. Especially when the money from the ticket sales is going to buy a new air conditioner for the church."

"I'm sure I can figure out another way to raise the money," Chance said. "But we can't do a musical called *Cowboy Scrooge* without a Scrooge. And not one person showed up to audition for the part." Which seemed strange. There had to be one person in town who wanted the part. Of course, Chance should count it as a blessing. This gave him the perfect excuse to cancel the show.

Unfortunately, these three women were not letting go of their Christmas tradition so easily.

"There has to be someone who could do it." Kitty looked at Hester with wide eyes. "Can you think of anyone, Witchy Woman? Anyone who might be the perfect Scrooge for the reverend—I mean our little play?"

Hester touched the amethyst crystal that hung around her neck. "There is someone who comes to mind. If we can talk her into doing it."

"Her?" Chance said.

"Do you have a problem with a female Scrooge, Reverend?" Mrs. Moody gave him a censoring look. "Little Cindy Evans tried out for Tiny Wrangler Tim."

Cindy Evans hadn't really wanted to try out. She'd been dragged down the aisle of the church kicking and screaming by her mother. She had then proceeded to glare at Chance, Kitty, and Hester the entire time she sang the song entitled "Sweet Tiny Wrangler Tim." When it was over, she stuck her tongue out at them and marched back down the aisle. But since she was the only child in town who had shown up to play Tiny Tim, she was a shoo-in. Chance could only imagine what she'd be like in rehearsals if he couldn't talk these women out of doing the show.

"I don't have a problem with a woman playing Scrooge," he said. "But if she didn't show up tonight, I doubt she wants the part."

"She couldn't show up," Hester said. "Everly's working tonight."

Chance dropped the water bottle he'd just picked up and it bounced a few times before rolling under the pew. "Everly?"

"Everly!" Kitty echoed him, dramatically. Obviously, she was getting ready for her part as Ghost of Christmas Present. "Of course. Why didn't I think of her? With that sweet-as-an-angel's voice, she would make the perfect lead for our play. And she has a little grumpy Scrooge in her too. She doesn't put up with any nonsense from drunk cowboys at Nasty's." She shook her head. "It will be a cryin' shame when that girl leaves town. Just a cryin' shame, I tell you."

"It certainly will be." Hester glanced over at Chance. "Wouldn't you agree, Reverend?"

He cleared his throat. "I don't think Everly will fit the part of Scrooge. She's too—"

"Good-lookin' as all get-out?" Kitty said.

Chance blinked. "I was going to say young."

"She's that too. And she's good-lookin'. And sassy. And the type of woman who can make a man forget—"

Hester cut her off. "I don't think we need to go into detail, Kitty. Everly will make a perfect Cowboy Scrooge."

"I agree." Mrs. Moody turned to Chance. "Now all you need to do is convince her."

He stared at her. "You want me to convince her?"

"That *would* be a director's job."

Having Everly in the play was the last thing he wanted. Or needed. He had enough trouble keeping her out of his thoughts. He didn't need to see her three times a week for rehearsals.

"Even if I can convince her to be Scrooge," he said. "I'm sure she won't be able to take off from Nasty Jack's to rehearse."

"Oh, we've already worked that—" Kitty cut off. "I mean I'm sure we could work that out. We could change one of the rehearsal nights to Sunday when the bar is closed. And the other two nights, I'm sure Wolfe would be happy to handle the bar for the couple hours Everly is rehearsing. Or Hayden if Gretchen decides to go into labor early." She grinned her bucktoothed grin. "Buckinghorse Palace is going to be brimming with babies for the holidays. First, sweet little Danny. And now precious little Theodore. Lily's daddy, Theo, and her stepmama, Vivian, showed me pictures of Teddy when I delivered their mail this morning. He has a thick cap of black hair just like his mama, but a stubborn chin just like his daddy."

Shane had texted Chance a picture of Stetson grinning from ear to ear as he cradled the blanket-wrapped newborn. It had been difficult to look at. He and Lori had wanted children. They had even picked out names.

"Then it's settled," Mrs. Moody cut into his thoughts. "Everly Grayson will be Scrooge." She smiled at Chance. "I have complete faith that you'll be able to convince her, Reverend Ransom."

Chance had zero faith he could persuade her. Everly would want to be in a Christmas musical as much as he wanted to direct one. Which is why he decided not to argue. That and these three women reminded him of his grandmother—probably because of their strong wills—and he had never been able to argue with Granny Ran.

"Fine. I'll talk to her."

The three women exchanged satisfied looks. If Chance didn't know better, he would have thought that they were in cahoots. But that was ridiculous. They couldn't have foreseen that no one would show up to audition for Scrooge.

⁂

The following morning, Chance wasted no time getting up and heading to Nasty Jack's. The sooner Everly declined the role, the sooner he could put a stop to the Christmas musical.

In his hurry to be rid of his directing job, he didn't think about the time until Everly answered the door with sleepy eyes, mussed hair, and dressed in boxer shorts and the shorty tank top that showed way too much of her stomach and cleavage. Thankfully, the three kittens wiggling in her arms blocked his view of both.

"Where did you get—"

She cut him off. "Don't ask. Do you have coffee and donuts?"

"Uhh . . . no."

The door slammed in his face.

He waited for it to reopen. It didn't. So he turned and headed back to his truck. When he returned with the coffee and donuts, he didn't knock. He balanced the tray in one hand and opened the door. He found Everly in her room facedown on her bed. The tiger-striped kitten seemed to be attacking her hair. The black one with the white front stockings was sitting on the top of the headboard, batting at the cord to the blinds. And the white one with the black mustache was soundly sleeping on a pillow.

"Everly?"

"You better have donuts and coffee." Her voice came through the hair covering her face. "And poison Meow Mix."

He laughed. "Sorry, no Meow Mix, but I do have coffee and donuts."

Her hair fluffed out as she heaved a sigh. "Then get this beast out of my hair."

He set the tray on the dresser, then walked over to the bed. The kitten had gotten itself thoroughly entangled in Everly's hair, and in order to free it, Chance had to sit on the bed and work the strands from its tiny claws and teeth. It was hard to focus on the task when memories of being in this same bed with this same woman wavered at the edge of his mind. It was a relief when the kitten was free.

He quickly got off the bed and moved a few

feet away as Everly sat up and smoothed back her hair.

Her eyes narrowed at the kitten Chance held. "And I thought you were the nice one, Flounder."

"Flounder?"

Everly rolled her eyes. "It seems Delaney has a horrible sense of humor. And a weird preoccupation with fairytales. She named her goats after the dwarfs and these kittens after *The Little Mermaid* movie."

"And just why do you have Delaney's cats?"

"Because Lily decided to go into labor when your brother was on his way to town to find homes for these demons." She reached out and caught the black kitten as it tumbled off the headboard. "Shane is now on my shit list." She held the kitten in front of her. "Isn't that right, Scuttle?" She kissed it right on the nose before she set it on the pillow next to the white kitten. "Don't wake Sebastian or I'll hang you up by your cute little ears." She got out of bed and headed for the coffee on the dresser.

Chance stepped out of her way. "So I take it you didn't find them homes."

"I haven't really had time to look." She took a sip of coffee and sighed before digging in the bag. Once she had a donut, she turned to him. "You're holding Flounder wrong. She likes to be cradled under her belly."

Chance adjusted the cat in his arms and lifted his brows at Everly. "Are you sure these kittens haven't already found a home?"

"I'm positive. I don't want anything to do

with these three demons. Scuttle pooped in my boot." She took a bite of donut. "Which wouldn't have been bad if I'd known about it before I slid my foot in." Chance cringed. "Exactly. It was definitely cringeworthy. And Sebastian snores." She pointed the donut at Flounder. "And that one has a thing for my hair."

Chance could understand why. Even messed, it looked like tempting flames.

"Nope," Everly continued. "I don't want, or need, three ornery kittens. Which is why I'm glad you showed up today, Preach. I figure it's a preacher job to take care of orphans."

"Oh, no." He held the kitten out. "You're not pawning them off on me."

"Why not?" She took Flounder and cradled her close. "It was your brother who pawned them off on me."

"That's between you and Shane. I have enough to worry about with the Christmas musical. Which is why I'm here. Kitty and Hester want you to be Cowboy Scrooge."

Everly lowered the donut she had just been about to take a bite of. "What?"

"No one showed up to audition for the part of Cowboy Scrooge so Hester and Kitty want you to do it."

"No one showed up? Like not one single person?"

"I found that strange too. But no. Now do you want the part or not?"

"Absolutely not." She took a big bite of donut. Some flakes of glazed icing fell off and landed on her breast. And not just on her breast, but on the jagged crack that ran down the middle of the deep red heart tattoo. When Shane had first introduced them, the tattoo had been right there for all to see and Chance had had a problem keeping his eyes off it.

Things hadn't changed.

"Something wrong with my boob, Preach?"

He lifted his gaze to see her smug smile. "I was looking at your tattoo."

She glanced down at the tattoo. "I'm sure people think Shane is responsible for it. He broke my heart so I raced out and got a tattoo."

Chance would have thought the same thing if he hadn't known better. She'd had the tattoo long before she'd fallen for Shane. "So who is responsible?"

She lifted her gaze. "It has nothing to do with a guy. I got it right after I ran away from home. I had big plans to become a tattoo artist, but then passed out the first time I punctured someone's skin with the tattoo pen. When I got the heart, I had to be heavily sedated with tequila. It's my one and only tat."

He was surprised. He thought she'd have a lot more . . . in places you couldn't see. "So why a broken heart?"

"That's a good question." She hesitated as if giving it some thought. "I guess I was feeling sad about running away from home. I was just seventeen and scared and lonely."

"Then why didn't you just go back?"

"Because I couldn't be what my parents wanted me to be."

"And what was that?"

"Perfect." She smiled, but it didn't reach her eyes. The deep amber held pain. He had always seen Everly as such a tough woman. This peek at her vulnerability completely broadsided him.

"No one is perfect, Everly."

She turned away to set the half-eaten donut down on the dresser. When she turned back, the vulnerable woman was gone. "Thus says the preacher who probably has made very few mistakes in his life. I, on the other hand, have made more than my fair share."

"You know what my Granny Ran used to say when I would make a stupid mistake and was feeling down on myself? She'd say 'The only one who doesn't make mistakes is God. Therefore, you can make all the mistakes in the world, but never think for one second that you're a mistake.'"

She smiled. "I loved Granny Ran."

Chance stared at her. "You met her?"

"Of course I met her. After Shane told me all about her, I had to meet her. He drove me out to her trailer and she taught me how to make pumpkin bread in a coffee can. Best pumpkin bread I've ever tasted."

The memory of his grandmother's coffee-can pumpkin bread brought tears to his eyes. Before he could blink them away, Everly placed a hand on his arm.

"I was so sorry when Shane told me about Granny Ran's passing. She was the kind of parent

I wished I'd had. Kind, loving, and so proud of you and Shane."

He swallowed the lump in his throat. "She was proud. She was especially proud of me becoming a pastor. She'd be disappointed if she could see me now."

"What are you talking about? Don't tell me you're still beating yourself up for getting a little drunk and kissing me. It wasn't that big of a sin, Preach."

"I'm not talking about the other night."

"Then what are you talking about?"

He didn't know why he told her the truth. He hadn't even told Shane. But for some reason, he felt like his secret would be safe with her.

"I'm talking about losing my faith. I can't believe in a god who would take the only two women I've ever loved."

# Chapter Seven

Everly startled awake. She squinted at the sun shining in through the window, wondering what had awakened her. Needlelike claws sinking into her head answered the question.

"Oww!" She reached behind her and grabbed Flounder. She started to scold the little devil, but it was hard to scold something that looked back at you with a cute face and wide blue eyes. Everly ended up kissing her on the furry head. "I'm such a sucker."

All three kittens were still with her. Mystic had volunteered to help her find homes for the cats. She had taken pictures of the kittens and printed up a flyer to put on the bulletin board in her salon. With the holidays so close, Everly had immediately started getting calls from people who wanted a kitten as a Christmas gift for their kids.

Unfortunately, they only wanted one kitten.

Everly just couldn't bring herself to split up the cats. She knew what it was like to be separated from a sibling. She couldn't do it to the kittens.

So she had added a note to the flyer. *PACKAGE DEAL! ALL THREE FOR FREE!*

There had been no more calls.

Until she found someone willing to adopt all three, she had been forced to purchase a few things from Amazon. Like three little beds so they'd stop sleeping in hers, and a litter box so they'd quit using her shoes, a scratching post so they wouldn't claw her hair and the furniture, a dozen little balls and toys so they'd leave her things alone, and a cat condo so they'd be able to look out the front window after she'd spent hours scraping all the black paint off.

The spare bedroom now looked like cat heaven.

And still the little pains-in-her-butt preferred her room to theirs.

She set Flounder on the pillow next to her and waved a hand. "Shoo, you pest. Go attack your brothers and leave me alone."

Flounder stared at her for a second before pouncing straight on her head.

Everly sighed. "A great, big sucker."

She allowed Flounder her fun for a few more minutes before she got up. As she headed to the bathroom, Scuttle came out of the closet—where he was no doubt using one of Everly's shoes—and Sebastian came out from under the bed with dust balls clinging to his white fur. All three kittens followed her to the bathroom where they unraveled an entire roll of toilet paper while she showered. After cleaning up the mess, she got dressed in yoga pants, a tank top, and her hot pink Nikes and headed downstairs where she fed the kittens and made herself coffee and a slice of pumpkin pie with a pile of whipped cream on top. Once the kittens had finished eating, she loaded them into the pet carrier.

Last night, she'd had an epiphany. Maybe she could bribe someone to take the kittens by including all the cat paraphernalia. She was going to ask Mystic if she'd make up another flyer with a list of everything Everly had purchased.

As soon as she stepped out of the bar, a cold wind smacked her in the face. It looked like fall had finally arrived in Texas just in time for Thanksgiving, which was only a few days away.

Delaney, Shane, Wolfe, and Gretchen had invited her to come to the ranch for dinner, but she'd declined the offer. While the Kingmans had always been welcoming, she still felt awkward when she was around the entire family. She planned on heading to Dallas for her two days off—the bar would be closed Thursday and Friday—and having Thanksgiving with friends. She'd booked a hotel that took pets. She only hoped the kittens would behave so she'd get back her pet deposit.

After making sure the door of the bar was locked, she headed across the street. The Malones' house was all decorated for the holiday. Gold and orange mums bloomed in the flowerbeds along the porch railing, groups of pumpkins and lanterns lined the porch steps, and a huge fall wreath hung on the front door.

A stab of sadness pierced Everly's heart. It happened occasionally. Usually when something reminded her of home. Her mother had always loved decorating their house for every holiday. There had been pumpkins and harvest wreaths for Thanksgiving, lights and shiny ribbon wreaths for Christmas, and faux lawn bunnies and spring flower wreaths for Easter. Her childhood house had been the prettiest on the block. Her mother and father had made sure of it.

William and Megan Grayson were perfectionists. Everything in their lives had to be perfect. Their house. Their lawn. Even their daughters. Or at least one daughter had been perfect.

Everly's older sister, Paisley, had gotten straight As and had said "yes, ma'am" and "no, sir" when spoken to. She had won trophies for track, debate, and memorizing the most Bible verses. She had married the most popular boy in their small Texas town and become a devoted wife and mother.

And then there was Everly.

At first, she had tried to be perfect. She had tried to like the stiff dresses and tight curls and outrageously huge hair bows her mother dressed her in. She had tried to excel at ballet and piano and whatever else her mother thought a young lady should know. She had kept her clothes clean, her comments polite, and her smile pretty. But when she hit eighth grade, she just hadn't been able to keep up the perfect façade a second longer.

When the real Everly busted out, she did so with a bang.

She went total grunge, buying her clothes at thrift stores and ripping holes in the oversized jeans and splattering paint on the T-shirts. She shaved the sides of her hair and dyed the rest a multitude of colors. She pierced her nose, lip, and ears—multiple times—and her belly button. She stopped doing well in school and started ditching class with a group of kids who drank, smoked pot, and cussed.

Her parents had been stunned. They took her to counselor after counselor, sent her away to summer camps for troubled kids, put locks on every window and door to try to keep her from sneaking out, tried to bribe her with money and the promise of a brand-new car if she could only pull it together.

But nothing could make Everly into the daughter they wanted.

So when Everly was seventeen, she figured it was better for everyone—her sister Paisley included—to leave. She had been home only once since leaving. It had been an awkward and tense visit. Paisley had still been perfect and Everly still hadn't been. Nor would she ever fit into the mold her parents wanted her to fit into.

Her heart was still broken over it.

But she wasn't about to let her family ruin the rest of her life.

Pushing the melancholy feelings away, she headed around the porch to the salon. But before she could get there, Kitty Carson's mail truck zipped into the parking lot and came to a gravel-spitting stop inches from her.

"Hey, Everly!" Kitty jumped out of the truck. "Everyone is just pleased as punch that you're going to be Cowboy Scrooge in our Christmas musical. With you in the lead, I think this year's performance is going to be the best yet. Barney could act better than Tom Hanks, but his singing talents left something to be desired. But you sing like an angel. A sweet angel."

Everly stared at Kitty. "I'm afraid there's been a misunderstanding. I didn't agree to be Cowboy Scrooge."

Kitty's eyes widened. "What? Well, that's strange. I thought Reverend Ransom told Mrs. Moody that you said yes."

*Chance had told everyone she was going to be in the musical?* That sounded suspicious. Chance didn't want to do the play either. Before she could get to the bottom of it, Kitty spied the kittens. They had found the flap in the side of the carrier and all three of their heads were poking out.

"Oh, would you look at these sweethearts?" Kitty stroked each furry head. "How's the search for a good kitten home going?"

"Not well. You wouldn't be interested, would you? I'll give you everything you need for their care. I'm talking a cat condo, beds, this carrier, and—"

Kitty cut her off. "Oh, I can't have pets. My mama is allergic." She winked. "And it looks like they're quite content right where they are."

Everly shook her head. "Oh, no, they're not content. I'm a horrible kitten mama. I'd sure appreciate it if you'd spread the word on your route about how cute they are. I need to find them a home before I leave. Together. They can't be separated."

"I'll be happy to, but I hope you're not in any hurry to leave. We can't have our Scrooge running off before the performance."

"But I'm not—"

"Gossiping again, Gossip Girl?"

Everly turned to see Hester Malone standing on her front porch. With the wind blowing back her long silver hair and waving her black skirt, she looked like the witch Kitty called her.

"I'm not gossiping, Witchy Woman. I was just thanking Everly for joining the cast of *Cowboy Scrooge*. This year, we're going to bring down the house." Before Everly could explain that she wasn't joining the cast, Kitty hopped back in her truck and waved. "See you two later. I'll be sure to spread the word about those kittens, Everly. If anyone can find them a good home, I can." She zipped the truck in a U-turn and took off.

When she was gone, Everly turned to Hester. "I'm not going to be Scrooge."

Hester studied her with her penetrating violet eyes. "Why don't you come inside for a cup of tea? It's much too windy out here."

Everly knew what the woman was up to. She planned to get her inside and convince her to be in the musical. But it wasn't going to happen. Unfortunately, before she could decline the offer, Flounder somehow wiggled out of the open flap in the carrier and jumped to the ground.

"Flounder!" Everly went to pick up the kitten, but Flounder streaked up the porch steps and through the open door Hester was holding. And maybe it wasn't a bad thing. Voodoo queen or not, Hester might be just the person to take the kittens off Everly's hands. Didn't witches love cats?

Everly climbed the steps and followed Flounder into the house.

The only way to describe the inside of the Malones' house was cozy. The house was brand new, but it looked like Hester had kept most of the old furniture the townsfolk had given her after the tornado swept the house away.

She led Everly to the overstuffed sofa sitting in front of the fireplace where a fire crackled and popped. "I have a pot of chai tea made, but I also have a variety of herbal if you'd prefer."

"Chai is good." She walked over to pick up Flounder before she got into something, but Hester stopped her.

"She's fine. You can let the other ones out too. Wish is at the salon with Mystic."

Everly had forgotten about Mystic's cat. She didn't want the kittens around the scary-looking black cat. She'd have to find another home for them. Even if the kittens seemed to love the house. As soon as she set down the carrier, Scuttle and Sebastian jumped out of the flap and joined their sister in investigating the room.

Hester returned shortly with a tray and set it down on the coffee table. Once she'd poured them each some tea, she settled back on the sofa with her cup. "So you don't want to be our Cowboy Scrooge."

"I'm sorry, but no. I'm sure you can find someone who would be much better at the part."

She picked up her cup and took a sip to be polite. She wasn't a tea drinker. But it turned out to be the best tea she'd ever tasted. It was spicy and rich and comforting. She took another sip and tried to relax. But it was hard to relax when Hester was studying her so intently.

"But Chance doesn't need another Scrooge. He needs you."

Everly halted with the teacup inches from her mouth. "Excuse me?"

"Chance needs you." Hester glanced down at the kittens that were playing with the tassels on the area rug. "As much as these kittens do."

Everly didn't want to talk about Chance. She'd spent the last couple weeks doing way too much thinking about him and the truth he'd shared with her. She knew he was struggling to get through his grief. She also knew that he hadn't wanted the job at Holy Gospel. But she hadn't thought he didn't want any pastoring job. She hadn't thought he'd lost his faith.

She set her cup down on the tray. "The kittens don't need me. And I'm the last person Chance needs. He doesn't even like me. He thinks the only reason I came here was to seduce his brother away from Delaney." Which was probably the only reason he was still in town.

"I don't think he feels that way anymore. Chance just doesn't like anyone right now. Not even himself. That's what happens when you lose your faith."

Everly stared at her. "He told you?"

Hester smiled as she set down her cup of tea.

"No. I saw it." She looked at Everly with her piercing eyes. "Just like I saw you as his savior."

Okay, this was getting weird. Hester was a nice woman and Everly didn't want to hurt her feelings, but she wasn't about to go along with this hocus-pocus craziness.

"I get it," she said. "Like everyone else in this town, you don't want to break tradition and cancel the Christmas musical. You think pulling a little voodoo fortune-telling is the way to get me to be Scrooge. But I don't believe in psychic powers and crystal balls. I believe in reality. The reality is that Chance isn't ready to direct a Christmas play. Or even pastor a church. Shane shouldn't have pushed him into it by pretending to—" She cut off, realizing what she was about to say. No one in town knew about the twin switch.

But it turned out that someone in town did.

"You're right," Hester said. "Shane shouldn't have applied for the pastoring job for his brother." When Everly looked at her with surprise, she smiled. "Yes, I knew Shane wasn't a preacher as soon as I met him."

"And you didn't tell the church board?"

"I was going to, but then I met Chance. I knew immediately he was the right man for the job. He's a good man with a good heart." Hester studied Everly. "Just like I knew the first time we met that you're a good woman with a good heart. Even though you try so hard to hide it."

"I don't hide anything. What you see is what you get."

"Is it?" Hester touched the amethyst stone

hanging from a chain around her neck. "I see a rebellious woman who works hard not to fit into any molds." She paused. "But not fitting in is a lonely road to follow."

"I'm not lonely. I don't need anyone and no one needs me. Not kittens. Or preachers. Or a Christmas musical." She stood. "Now if you'll excuse me, I need to have your granddaughter print me out a new free kitten flyer."

Hester released the amethyst and nodded. "Of course." She patted her lap. As if by magic—or some voodoo spell—first one kitten, and then the other, stopped playing with the tassels and hopped up on Hester's lap. She closed her eyes and stroked the kittens. "You'll find a home for these three. A home where they will feel loved and cherished. A home that will have children. Three children to love their three cats."

She opened her eyes and looked up at Everly. "It *will* be a perfect home."

# Chapter Eight

CHANCE HAD ALWAYS hated being sick and having to stay in bed. When he'd been a child, he'd tried to hide his symptoms from his grandmother so she wouldn't make him stay home from school. But when he woke up on Thanksgiving morning with a fever, all he felt was relief. Shane had invited him to dinner at the Kingman Ranch and the fever gave him the perfect excuse for not going. It would be too hard to smile and keep up the conversation when all he would be thinking about was his last Thanksgiving with Lori.

She had woken him up with a kiss, followed by a morning of making love. While the turkey was cooking, they'd gone kayaking on Lady Bird Lake. They'd stayed too long and returned home to a burned turkey so they'd made hot dogs to go with their side dishes. As he'd bent his head over the odd feast, Chance had thanked God for his wonderful life and beautiful wife.

Today, he didn't feel thankful.

After he made his excuses to Shane, he went back to bed. When he woke a few hours later, he was burning with fever and every muscle in his body ached. He should get up and take some flu medicine, but he couldn't find the energy. And what did it matter? There was no one to get up for. He didn't know how long he lay there feeling miserable before the doorbell rang.

He tried to ignore it. But whoever it was refused to go away. Figuring it was Shane checking up on him, he rolled out of bed and made his way to the door. But it wasn't Shane standing on his front stoop.

It was Everly.

If he hadn't felt so bad, he might have been embarrassed about standing there in nothing but his boxer briefs. Especially when Everly gave him a thorough once-over.

She sighed. "I guess I lost the bet. I thought for sure you were lying when Shane told me you were sick."

"Is that why you're here? To prove I lied?"

"Pretty much." She leaned in and pressed a cool hand to his forehead. It felt way too good to pull away. "Yep. I lost the bet. You're sick. Which means you have no business standing here in the doorway in your sexy undies." She pushed her way inside, took him by the shoulders, and turned him in the direction of his room. "Let's get you back to bed."

He was too weak to argue. Once he was in bed, she tucked him in like he was a three-year-old, then headed for the bathroom. He heard cabinet doors opening and closing. A few minutes later, she reappeared with a glass of water and a bottle of cold and flu medicine. She handed him the water before shaking out three capsules from the bottle. Once he'd taken them and downed all the water, she took the empty glass and patted him on the head.

"Good boy. Now get some rest." She turned and walked out of the room. When he heard the front door open and then close, he figured she'd left.

He fell asleep thinking about her cool hand on his forehead. Which explained why he dreamed about her. It was a strange dream. She was bathing him with a cool, damp cloth and yelling at demons to get away. Strangely, he felt safe in her care, like as long as she was there, the demons that had haunted him for so long would stay away.

But they didn't.

The dream shifted and it wasn't Everly who was bathing him, but Lori. She was smiling at him like she had the very first time he'd met her. A soft, shy smile that made her look like the Madonna. She stroked him with the cool cloth and spoke in a gentle voice.

"It's okay. You can let go now."

But he didn't want to let go. He wasn't ready. He reached out and pulled her into his arms and held tightly as he buried his face in her neck.

"Don't leave me. Please don't leave me."

Her arms came around him and rubbed his back in soothing caresses. "Okay, Preach. I won't leave."

Sometime later, he awoke feeling disoriented and feverish. He tried to roll over to get into a more comfortable position, but something was pinning him to the mattress. He opened his eyes. It was dark in the room, but he recognized the pile of red hair spilling across his bare chest. Everly's hand rested over his heart and her warm breath brushed his skin with each exhale. On his stomach, three balls of fur were curled together, purring softly.

Chance closed his eyes and went back to sleep.

When he woke again, sunlight was shining through the closed slats of the blinds. He glanced down. The fiery-haired woman and kittens were gone. He wondered if he had dreamed it. Or possibly hallucinated it because of his fever. He didn't feel feverish now. He felt hungry and thirsty. A glass of water sat on the nightstand, along with a new bottle of Tylenol. He took a couple tablets and downed the water before heading to the bathroom.

He stayed in the shower for a long time, allowing the steam to clear his head and the hot spray to massage his achy muscles. He was about to turn off the faucet and get out when the door opened and Everly waltzed in.

"You okay, Preach?"

He quickly turned toward the tiled wall. "What are you doing? I'm showering."

"So I see . . . although I can't really see. You mind swiping some of that moisture off so I can get a better view?"

"Everly," he said in his sternest voice.

She laughed. "Don't get your panties in a bunch.

I just wanted to make sure you're okay. But from what I can see, you're more than okay."

"Everly."

"Fine. I'll leave you to shower alone . . . regardless of how nice your ass looks behind that steamed-up glass." The door clicked closed.

Chance wasted no time getting out and drying off. Tucking the towel securely around his waist, he stepped out of the bathroom. For the first time, he noticed that his room had been straightened. The half-unpacked boxes and the pile of clean laundry were gone. When he looked in his dresser drawers, he found neatly folded stacks of clothing. In the closet, his boots and running shoes were now lined up under his organized shirts and suits. While he was standing there trying to get over the fact that Everly had cleaned his room, the smell of cooking bacon and brewing coffee tickled his nostrils. His stomach rumbled and he released the towel and dressed in some sweats.

He walked into the kitchen to find the breakfast nook table set with two plates filled with eggs, crispy bacon, and buttered toast.

"I didn't know how you took your eggs so you got them how I like them. Sunny-side up."

He turned to see her standing there with two mugs of coffee in her hands and three little kittens frolicking around her bare feet. She was dressed in yoga pants and a tank top. Her hair was messed and her makeup smudged. She looked like she had just rolled out of bed

His bed.

"You spent the night."

She handed him one of the mugs. "I didn't want to, but you refused to let me go." She shook her head. "You really need to make up your mind, Preach. First you want me to leave and then you beg me to stay." She took a sip of coffee and wrinkled her nose. "Damn, I hate pod coffee." She turned and headed to the table. "Well, don't just stand there. I didn't slave over a hot stove for it to get cold."

Chance shouldn't have been surprised that breakfast was delicious. He was learning Everly could do a lot of things well. Including organizing a cluttered room and taking care of sick people. After he finished breakfast, he glanced over at her.

"Thank you."

"No need to thank me. I just made too much for myself so I decided to share."

"I wasn't just thanking you for breakfast. Thank you for straightening my room . . . and for staying and taking care of me."

She smiled evilly. "I just want to score brownie points with Shane. I'm sure he'll be more willing to leave Delaney for a woman who nursed his brother back to health."

At one time, he would have believed it was part of her scheme to get his brother back. But now he wasn't so sure there was a scheme. If she was trying to get Shane back, she certainly hadn't put much time or effort into it. She'd been too busy with work and three mischievous kittens to pay any attention to his brother.

And yet, she had taken time to care for Chance. It confused him. If he had felt better, he would have questioned her motives. But the shower and breakfast had depleted his energy. As if sensing that, Everly gave him more cold tablets and shooed him back to bed. He slept the day away. When he woke, it was dark again.

But it wasn't quiet.

There was singing.

Beautiful singing.

"It's Beginning to Look a Lot Like Christmas" was ringing through the house in Everly's strong, clear voice. The townsfolk were right. She did belong in the Christmas musical. But he had no intentions of convincing her to do it. If they didn't find a Cowboy Scrooge in time for the first rehearsal on Sunday night, Mrs. Moody, Hester, and Kitty would have to accept the fact that the play needed to be cancelled.

He lay there listening to Everly sing for a few minutes before he got up. After using the bathroom, he brushed his teeth and tried to bring some order to his bed head. He felt much better. He knew he had Everly to thank. As soon as he finished brushing his hair, he followed her voice to the living room.

When he got there, he stopped short at the sight that greeted him.

Everly was decorating an artificial Christmas tree. And not just any tree, but the same tree he and Lori had bought their first Christmas together. She was decorating it with the vintage ornaments Lori had searched every thrift store in Austin for. He remembered the joy on her face when she found another antique Santa or reindeer or snowman. One of those snowmen was on the floor being batted around by the kittens.

The pain that speared through Chance almost doubled him over and he had to grab on to the back of the couch to steady himself. It took a few minutes before he could find his voice.

"Stop."

But Everly couldn't hear him over her loud singing.

When he felt like his shaking legs would support him, he released the couch and walked over to her. She cut off mid-verse and turned to him with a bright smile.

"You're alive, Preach."

"What are you doing?"

"What does it look like I'm doing? I'm decorating a Christmas tree." She went to put the ornament on the tree, but he grabbed it from her. The fragile glass broke in his hand.

He stared at the crack in the Santa's head. "Look what you've done,"

"What I've done? You were the one who broke it."

He lifted his gaze and his anger snapped. "And you were the one who went through boxes you had no business going through!"

"Well, pardon me, but I thought a few decorations would make your house less depressing and cheer you up. Obviously, I was wrong."

"It's not your business to make my house less depressing or cheer me up."

"You're right. But if it's not my business,

then whose business is it, Chance? You need help. You've done a great job of hiding how screwed up you are from your brother and your congregation. The only one you haven't hidden it from is Hester Malone and she's not going to help you because she's under some misconception that I'm your savior." She thumped her chest. "Well, I'm no savior. But, unfortunately, I can't sit back and let a man drown either. At least not without throwing him some kind of floatation device."

She grabbed the front of his sweatshirt in both her hands. He thought she was going to give him a hard shake. Instead, she jerked him closer and . . . kissed him. It wasn't a quick peck. It was a deep, wet, tongue-sweeping kiss. He didn't just feel the softness of her lips and the heat of her mouth and the brush of her tongue. He felt her energy. It flooded through him like a rush of electricity, awakening every cell in his body.

He felt alive.

And he wanted more of her life-giving force.

He wrapped his arms around her and tugged her closer. Chance might not remember the night they spent together at the bar, but his body seemed to. There was nothing awkward about the joining of their mouths. Their lips fit together perfectly and their tongues brushed in a heated waltz that left Chance dizzy with desire.

Then suddenly she stopped kissing him and pulled away.

Her lips were wet and her eyes whiskey glazed. He went to kiss her again, but she stopped him.

"No, Chance. I kissed you for one reason and

one reason only. To prove to you that you're alive." Her hands tightened on his shirt. This time, she did shake him. "You're alive, Chance Ransom. You're a living, breathing man with desires and needs. So start swimming, Preach. Stop drowning and start swimming." She released his sweatshirt and went back to decorating the tree and singing as if nothing had happened.

He felt shaken, and not because Everly was decorating Lori's tree. He felt shaken because she was right. He was alive. She had proven it. His body still hummed with need and desire. He still wanted to pull her back into his arms and continue kissing her.

Instead, he turned and walked out the front door. Once outside, he took deep breaths and tried to right his suddenly tipsy world. The broken ornament was still in his hand. He threw it as hard as he could before he looked up at the night sky and asked the one question he'd asked over and over again after losing Lori and his grandmother.

"Why?"

In Austin, the stars had struggled to compete with big-city lights. Here in Cursed, the stars had no competition and filled the deep void of the sky like intersecting highways of glittering diamonds. But there was no divine revelation spelled out in the sky. There was no deep voice explaining the unexplainable. There was just the twinkling stars and silence.

Then suddenly . . . there was an explosion of

light that lit up the dark and spilled across the lawn.

Chance turned.

A Christmas tree stood in the front window. A tree that looked nothing like the tree he and Lori had decorated their first Christmas together. They had only put two or three strings of lights on the tree. It looked like Everly had used every string of lights she had found—including the outdoor lights.

The tree was glowing like it was on fire.

And so was the woman standing next to it.

Everly's red hair and amber eyes reflected the lights as she looked at the tree. But instead of looking happy with her accomplishment, she looked sad. He couldn't ever remember Everly looking sad. She'd looked sassy. Smug. Flirtatious. Sexy.

But never sad.

For the first time, he realized he wasn't the only one suffering from a loss. He wasn't the only one struggling to get through the holidays. She had lost Shane. And not only that, she had lost her family. But while he refused to even make the effort, Everly was at least trying.

And not just for herself, but for him.

She startled as if something had pulled her out of her thoughts. She disappeared from the window and, a second later, she returned with her cellphone. Whoever she was talking with had brought her out of her sad mood. Her face lit up as bright as the tree. That was the thing about Everly. She never let anything keep her down for long. She disappeared from the window again and the front door flew open.

"Gretchen and Wolfe's baby decided to come early! Shane called and said Maribelle Adeline Kingman was born just moments ago." Everly smiled. "So it looks like you'll soon be rid of me, Preach."

# Chapter Nine

SINCE NASTY JACK'S had been closed two days for Thanksgiving, Saturday night was packed. With Wolfe and Gretchen at home with their new daughter, Everly had her hands full. Thelma and Otis were helping in the kitchen and Delaney and Shane were waiting tables, but Everly was the only one working the bar. As she raced from one end of the bar to the other taking drink orders, she wondered how Wolfe had ever handled weekend crowds by himself. It was a relief when Hayden showed up. Even though it was supposed to be his night off, he didn't hesitate to move behind the bar and start filling orders.

"Can you do everything?" Everly asked when she glanced over and saw him expertly mixing a lemon drop martini.

"Hey, I was a poor rodeo tramp. I had to get work where I could." He poured the drink and hung a curl of lemon peel on the side of the sugar-rimmed martini glass before setting it on the bar in front of a woman who hadn't taken her eyes off Hayden since she'd sat down.

"I need two tap beers and a bottle of Bud

Light." Shane squeezed his way up to the bar. "Hey, Hayden. I didn't know you were working tonight."

"Just helping Everly out."

Shane glanced between him and Everly and smiled. "That's real nice of you." He winked at Everly.

Everly shot him an annoyed look as she grabbed two beer glasses. "Don't go there, Shaney."

"Go where . . . " Shane's smile got even bigger. "Ebenezer. According to what I've been hearing, you're going to be the best Cowboy Scrooge ever."

Everly had been hearing the same thing all night long. Apparently, Hester hadn't made things clear to Kitty. Or anyone else. The entire town thought Everly was going to be the new lead in the Christmas musical.

"Well, you've heard wrong. I'm not going to be Scrooge. I just haven't had time to make that clear to everyone. Although they'll figure it out when I don't show up to the first rehearsal tomorrow night."

"Oh, come on, Ev. Don't be such a . . . Scrooge."

Everly rolled her eyes. "Very funny."

Shane laughed. "Sorry, bad joke. But seriously, why don't you do it? You love to sing and weren't you in *Hamlet* in college?"

"Only because I fell for the guy playing Hamlet. I wanted to be his Ophelia. Instead I got cast as his mother."

Shane grinned. "And if I remember correctly, the guy still asked you out."

"Sadly. He turned out to be much better at acting than he was at carrying on a conversation that didn't include hours of talking about himself. Which ended my infatuation with actors."

"You then went on to be infatuated with guys who played in cover bands."

She'd forgotten about her band groupie stage. "They were just as self-absorbed as actors. I don't know how many dates I spent filming my boyfriends' performances so they could critique them later."

Which was how she had ended up with a different infatuation.

Shane.

Shane hadn't been self-absorbed. He'd been sweet and kind and genuinely cared about what Everly was thinking and feeling. After their night of drunk sex, Everly had been convinced that all Shane needed was time to realize they were more than just friends. They were a perfect couple. Once he got the app he was developing launched and made his first million, he would be ready to settle down and have a serious relationship.

She'd waited. And waited. And waited. Then one day, he'd met a cowgirl princess and Everly's waiting was over. So was her dream of marrying Shane. And as she stood there looking at him, she had to wonder if he had just been another one of her infatuations. Another man she expected to fill the void inside her.

An image of Chance popped into her head.

She shouldn't have put up the Christmas tree. That had been way out of line. It had just been so sad walking into the garage and finding all those boxes labeled with the letter *L* and then whatever the box contained: her clothes, her shoes, her pictures, her Christmas decorations. Everly had thought it might help Chance if she took the decorations out of the box. But the pain in his eyes when he'd seen the tree had made her realize he wasn't ready to move on.

Still, she'd made one last—stupid—ditch effort to pull him from his grief.

What had she been thinking, kissing him? The kiss hadn't proven anything to Chance. But it had proven something to her. Tequila hadn't made Chance's kisses seem better than they were.

His kisses totally rocked her world.

"Man, it's crazy tonight." Delaney stepped up to the bar and handed Everly a drink order. "And you two standing here yakking isn't helping things."

Shane tucked an arm around Delaney and tugged her close. "Now don't get feisty, sugar pea. I was just trying to talk Everly into being Cowboy Scrooge."

Delaney turned to Everly. "You're not going to be Cowboy Scrooge? But that's all anyone can talk about tonight. The women of this town are damn excited about having our first female Scrooge."

"Sorry," Everly said. "But I'm too busy with the bar and the three kittens you pawned off on me. Sebastian, Scuttle, and Flounder are probably destroying my room as we speak—the little demons."

Shane took the beers Everly had just finished filling and set them on a tray. "Admit it, you've fallen in love with those demons."

"I certainly have not. It would be stupid to fall in love with them when they'll be adopted by a wonderful family soon—Hester has seen it."

Delaney stared at her. "You're really not going to keep the kittens?"

Everly smiled brightly, even though talking about giving the kittens away had started to make her feel extremely depressed. "Nope. There's no way an apartment landlord will let me keep three fur balls."

Delaney and Shane exchanged looks before Delaney spoke. "But you can't go back to Dallas, Everly. Gretchen and Wolfe need you. And so does Shane. He needs a friend to complain to about his nagging wife. If he complains to my brothers, they'll punch him. And Chance likes me too much to put up with Shane bad-mouthing me."

"She's right, Ev," Shane said. "Chance refuses to listen to me complain about my horribly mean wife who works my butt off trying to save every abused and neglected animal in Texas."

Delaney turned to him. "Hey, I wasn't the one who brought home that ornery mule."

"Desmond isn't ornery. He's just struggling to fit in." He glanced at Everly. "Like Ev, here. I thought she was a big city woman, but it turns out she's really a small town girl. In Dallas, she was uptight and anxious. Here, she's much more relaxed and happy."

"Happy?" Everly opened a beer. "How can I be happy when I'm working my butt off six days a week, have three devilish kittens to find a home for, and am being hounded to be Cowboy Scrooge when I've never even been on a horse?"

"We can remedy that," Delaney said. "Shane didn't know how to ride either when he got here. Now he's almost as good as my brothers at riding."

Shane smiled proudly. "I have to be when the woman who stole my heart is the best cowgirl on both sides of the Pecos." He and Delaney exchanged looks that pretty much said they were crazy about each other.

Everly rolled her eyes as she set the bottle of beer on Shane's tray. "I swear I just threw up in my mouth. If you two are through drooling over each other, Shane needs to deliver his drinks."

Shane winked at Delaney. "We'll continue this later, sugar pea." He picked up his tray and headed back to the tables.

When he was gone, Everly looked at Delaney. "Congratulations, you have turned a fairly normal guy into a lovesick sap."

Delaney grinned. "I have, haven't I? And speaking of sick guys, Shane told me about you nursing Chance back to health."

She started filling glasses with ice. "I wouldn't say I nursed Chance back to health. I just handed out a few cold meds and made him breakfast after we woke up." She realized her mistake when Delaney's eyes widened.

"You stayed the night with Cha—"

Since she was talking loud enough for the entire bar to hear, Everly quickly slapped a hand over her mouth. The people sitting closest turned and stared and she smiled. "Del was just about to say a cuss word and you know how the Kingmans hate their little sister cussing."

Everyone nodded their agreement before they went back to their conversations.

Everly thought Delaney would be pissed about her methods of shutting her up. But when Everly lowered her hand, Delaney was grinning. "Hmm? Very interesting. First, you nurse him back to health. And now you're protecting his good name."

"You know what would happen if word got out. He could get fired." And that was the last thing Chance needed. Everly might not agree with Hester about being his savior, but she did agree that he was a good man with a good heart. He just needed to get through his grief and get back his faith. The best place to do that was right here in Cursed.

"I doubt Chance would get fired," Delaney said. "Nobody seemed to care when Kitty spread it around town that she'd seen him coming home early in the morning after the wed—" She cut off. It was obvious by her widening eyes that she had just put two and two together. "It was you who—"

Thankfully, before Everly had to slap a hand over Delaney's mouth again, Hayden walked up.

"I think we might have a problem."

Everly followed his gaze down the bar and saw

a little boy sitting on a barstool. The kid couldn't be more than five. His chin barely reached the edge of the bar. Everly would have thought he was with some idiot parent who didn't know it was illegal to bring an underage kid into a bar if everyone around the boy wasn't looking at him with confusion.

"You want me to handle it?" Hayden asked.

Normally, she would have accepted the offer. She knew nothing about dealing with kids. But dealing with a child was better than dealing with Delaney and all the questions she would no doubt want to ask.

"No. I got it." She moved down the bar and stopped in front of the little boy. "Hey, cowboy. I think you might be in the wrong place."

The kid lifted his chin defiantly. "No, I'm not."

"So you just decided after you had supper and finished watching the Cartoon Network, you'd come to a bar—an adult bar?"

"I didn't habe supper tonight. I had Cheetos and a Snickers from the gas station me and Mama stopped at." He stood up on the rungs of the barstool and looked around the bar. "Now I'm lookin' for someone and you're ruptin' me."

Everly couldn't help but grin at the kid's audacity. "Well, I hate to interrupt anyone on a mission, but if you tell me your mama's name, I might be able to help you." She figured any kind of mother who would give their kid a Snickers and Cheetos for supper would also leave them in the car while they had a drink at a honky-tonk.

"It's not my mama I'm lookin' for." He

continued to scan the crowd. "She's in our Range Rober in the parking lot."

Everly was completely confused. "So your mama sent you in here by yourself to look for someone?"

"Yep. My mama said to look for a woman who has hair like a rainbow. And you don't habe hair like a rainbow."

"Hair like a rainbow?" Everly stared at the kid. There was only one woman in Cursed who had ever had hair like a rainbow. "Who is your mama, kid?"

"I can't tell you. My mama said to only talk to my Aunt Eberly."

Everly couldn't have been more stunned if the kid had punched her in the face. "You're Paisley's son? Henry?" The kid didn't have to answer. It was there in the surprised hazel eyes that looked back at her. Hazel eyes just like hers and her father's. She pointed a finger at Henry. "Stay right there. Don't move." She hurried back to Hayden. "I'll be back in a few minutes."

He looked concerned. "You need help? Shane or Delaney can watch the bar."

"Thanks. I got it." But by the time she made it around the bar, the kid was gone. After searching for him in the crowd, she hurried for the door. In the packed parking lot, it took her a while to find the Range Rover.

Instead of heading for it, she hesitated.

It had been years since she'd seen or talked with her older sister. Almost five to be exact. When they had been younger, they'd been close. But after Everly had stopped trying to meet their parents' expectations, she'd wanted nothing to do with her goody-goody sister. Paisley's perfection had only made their parents' rigid standards worse. Once she became an adult, Everly had realized her mistake. But it was too late. The chasm between the two sisters had been too wide to cross.

The last time she'd seen Paisley was when she'd gone back home after graduating college. Paisley had been married and was pregnant. She had still been their parents' perfect girl. She had married the son of the richest man in town and lived in a big mansion. Her blond hair and makeup had been flawless. Her clothes modest and impeccable. Everly had been dressed in cut-off jeans with rainbow hair, piercings, and tattoos. After sitting for two uncomfortable hours on her parents' front porch, she had realized she still didn't fit in with her family.

Which was why she was hesitant now. But there had to be a reason her sister had hunted her down. Whatever it was, it couldn't be good. The thought that her parents were sick, or even dead, had her feet finally moving. She might not be the perfect child they had wanted, but that didn't mean she didn't love them.

Fear filled her as she approached the Range Rover. It grew worse when she saw the woman sitting in the driver's seat next to Henry.

Gone was her perfectly coiffed sister. In her place was a woman with messed hair, mascara smudged beneath one eye, and red lipstick smeared across her bottom lip. It wasn't until the window rolled down that Everly realized it wasn't smudged mascara or smeared lipstick. Her sister's eye was bruised and her bottom lip split.

"Oh my God, Paise," Everly said. "What happened?"

Paisley sent her a wobbly smile. "I chose badly, Ev."

## Chapter Ten

First thing Sunday morning, Chance called the head of the church board and used the virus he'd contracted as an excuse to cancel morning services and the first musical rehearsal that night. By noon, get-well cards, cookies, and casseroles started arriving on his doorstep . . . making Chance feel extremely guilty about his ruse.

He wasn't sick anymore.

At least not physically.

Mentally was another story.

As he read each card, his guilt grew and he realized he couldn't keep up the charade of being the town's pastor a second longer. The good people of Cursed needed a strong, faithful man to guide them. They didn't need a weak, faithless one.

On Monday morning, he sat down and wrote his resignation. He was about to email it to the members of the church board when the doorbell rang. Fearing it was Everly, he ignored it. He wasn't ready to see her again. Their kiss had played over and over in his mind for the last two days. At one point, he'd even started to compare it with Lori's kisses. Which was all wrong.

"Chance!" Shane's voice came through the door.

Chance got up from his desk to answer it. When he opened the door, Shane's eyes widened. "What the hell, Chance? Every time I called to check on you, you kept telling me you weren't that sick."

"I'm fine. I just haven't shaved for a couple days." He held open the door for his brother.

"You sure—" Shane cut off when he stepped inside and saw the Christmas tree. He looked back at Chance and grinned. "I'm glad to see you're getting into the holiday spirit, bro. Does this mean I have to buy you a present?"

A few days ago, Chance would have joked back with Shane and continued to pretend like everything was okay. But he just didn't have it in him anymore. "I'm resigning from Holy Gospel."

Shane stared at him. "What? Why?"

"Because I'm a horrible pastor and the people of Cursed deserve better."

"You're not a horrible pastor. You're just grieving, is all. With a little time, you'll be your old self again." Shane waved at the tree. "That's a huge step."

"Everly put it up. Without my permission."

Shane's shoulders fell. "Oh." He heaved a sigh. "Well, I guess if you really don't want to be a pastor, that's your choice. But you'll stay in Cursed, right?"

Chance shook his head. "You don't need me putting a wet blanket on your happiness."

"You're part of my happiness, Chance. You're my brother. I want you in my life." He paused. "I want you in your niece's or nephew's life."

"Delaney's pregnant?"

Shane's smile was as bright as the sun shining in through the back French doors. "That's why I didn't come over when you were sick. I was worried about catching something and giving it to Delaney."

Chance couldn't deny being jealous, but he was also happy. He gave Shane a tight hug. "Congrats, Bro."

Shane hugged him back before he drew away. "Come on, Chance, stay. At least until after the holidays. There's no way the church board will be able to find another preacher before then and even a grieving pastor is better than no pastor at all."

Chance hesitated for a moment before he nodded. "Okay. I'll stay until after the holidays. But I'm not directing the musical."

"Why not? If you can deal with a Christmas tree in your house, you can deal with a little ol' Christmas musical."

He couldn't deal with the tree. It brought back memories every time he looked at it. And what was weird was that they weren't of Lori. They were of Everly and their kiss.

"Come on." Shane slapped him on the shoulder. "Let's go shoot some hoops."

As they played basketball in the driveway,

Shane caught him up on the Kingman family news. It seemed that Mystic was pregnant too. She and Buck had made the announcement at Thanksgiving dinner right after Shane and Delaney had made theirs. It looked like the castle would be brimming with babies.

"Hey, Ransom boys!"

Chance turned to see Everly walking down the street toward them. He hadn't seen her since Friday night. For some strange reason, his heart picked up at just the sight of her. She always looked like she just rolled out of bed in the mornings. But this morning, she looked like she hadn't had any sleep. He immediately grew concerned.

"Did you catch my virus? If so, you shouldn't be wandering around the streets. You need to be home in bed."

"I'm not sick. I'm here because I need help."

Shane handed the ball off to Chance. "What do you need, Ev?"

"Thanks, but I don't need your help, Shaney." She looked at Chance. "I need a pastor."

Chance didn't hesitate to hand the ball back to Shane. "Let me shower and change and I'll be right back."

"You don't need to change. In fact, looking less like a holier-than-thou preacher and more like an average guy might be better."

As soon as they said goodbye to Shane and were headed down the street toward Nasty Jack's, Chance turned to her. "Okay, what's going on?"

She gritted her teeth. "My big sister's asshole

husband used her as a punching bag. And it isn't the first time it's happened. But for the life of me, I can't get her to listen to reason and call the cops and press charges. That's where you come in. One of your jobs is to counsel people, right? I want you to talk to my sister and convince her to press charges so they can toss that friggin' abusive asshole into jail."

Chance had dealt with abuse cases before and the odds of him talking Everly's sister into pressing charges weren't good. Especially if she was as stubborn as Everly.

Surprisingly, Paisley Grayson Stanford wasn't anything like Everly. She was blond, soft-spoken, and extremely proper. When they were introduced, she held out a hand and acted like she was meeting him at a garden party instead of a small town honky-tonk ... with her eye bruised and her lip swollen.

"It's a pleasure to meet you, Reverend Ransom," she said. "Thank you so much for coming. But like I told Everly, I'm not interested in pressing charges against Jonathan."

"For, God sake's, Paise," Everly said as she paced the floor behind the bar where her sister sat. "The guy needs to be taught that he can't use you—or any woman—as his own personal punching bag."

"He knows that, Everly. He's always sorry after he hits me."

"Sorry! He's sorry? If he were sorry, he wouldn't keep doing it. I should go to Mesaville and kick his sorry ass from—"

Knowing a tirade wasn't going to help Paisley,

Chance cut in. "Everly, why don't you give me and your sister a few minutes alone." He thought she would argue, but instead she nodded.

"Fine. I probably need to go check on Henry anyway."

"Henry?"

"My sister's kid. When you're done convincing Paisley to pull her head out of her butt, come on up and I'll introduce you. He's spoiled rotten and too cocky, but kinda cute ... when he's not trying to bathe my demons in the toilet." It was the first time he'd heard her refer to the kittens as hers. He smiled as she walked away.

"My sister doesn't mince words, does she?"

He pulled his gaze from Everly's retreating back and looked at Paisley. "No, she doesn't? I've never met a more blunt woman in my entire life."

"And yet, you're friends."

He wanted to argue the point, but he couldn't. He didn't know how it had happened, but, somehow, he and Everly *had* become friends.

"You were the first person she mentioned this morning when she couldn't convince me to press charges," Paisley continued. "*Preach will talk some sense into you.*"

He studied the bruises on her face. "And can I?"

Her cheeks colored and she shook her head. "No. I won't press charges. But I can't go back either. I know that now."

Chance had talked with enough abused women to know the final straw usually had to do with their children. "Did he hurt Henry?"

Tears glistened in her eyes. They weren't Everly's amber gold. They were more greenish hazel. Pretty, but just not as pretty. "He was going to until I stepped in. Thankfully, he pulled me into the other room so Henry didn't have to witness what happened next. Henry just thinks his mother is clumsy."

Chance had to wonder if that was true. It was hard to hide things from children. "Even if you don't press charges, I would recommend taking pictures of your injuries. You might need them if there's a battle for custody."

She nodded. "You're right, but I'd be surprised if Jonathan wants anything to do with Henry. He never wanted children. I was the one who stupidly pushed to have one. I thought a child would make his anger better. It just seemed to make things worse."

Chance reached out and covered her hand that was resting on the bar. "Nothing you did, or didn't do, caused your husband to be an abuser. He needs help."

Paisley swallowed. "Deep down, I know that. But I still can't help blaming myself. I was the one who let it go on. I should've left the first time it happened." She looked at Chance. "I'm surprised you aren't pushing me to save my marriage. I thought pastors believed in the sanctity of wedding vows."

"There are times when you have to choose between your safety and that of your children's over the vows you make to your spouse. The way

I see it, your husband broke his vows first. He didn't love, honor, and cherish you."

She smiled sadly. "He did when we were dating. He treated me just like a princess. It wasn't until we got married that his temper started to show. I should've left him then, but I kept making excuses for his behavior. My parents had drilled it into my head that marriage was forever and you didn't quit when things got tough. Which is why I couldn't go to them. I know they would've just talked me into going back."

"I doubt they would've done that when they saw you."

"You don't know my parents. They spent their lives hiding anything that might take away from their perfect façade. Having an abusive son-in-law or a divorced daughter will not be acceptable. Have you seen the movie *Pleasantville*?"

"The one with Reese Witherspoon and Tobey Maguire?"

"That's the one. Our house was like the 1950s sitcom Reese's and Tobey's characters ended up in. Everything was picture perfect from our spotless house and immaculate lawn to the two little girls who lived there. Growing up, Everly and I were treated like dolls instead of children. We were dressed in frilly dresses and big bows and scolded for getting dirty or messing our hair. We were expected to play quietly and only speak when spoken to. It wasn't hard for me. I've always been shy and quiet. But it was hell for Everly. She wanted so much to please my parents and be a pretty, silent doll. But her true nature finally had to break free."

"And what happened when it did?"

"At first, my parents tried everything to get her to conform. When she wouldn't, they acted like she didn't exist." Once again, tears came to Paisley's eyes. "And I wasn't much better. I should've been a big sister and sided with Everly. I should've protected her and made her feel like there was nothing wrong with being her own person. Instead, I sided with our parents and made her feel like an outcast." She glanced around. "But it looks like she's not an outcast anymore." She smiled at him. "It looks like she's found people who accept her for who she is." She got up from the barstool. "Now I better go check on my son. It was nice meeting you, Reverend Ransom."

He stood. "It was nice meeting you too. And please call me Chance. If there's anything I can do for you or Henry while you're here, let me know."

"Thank you."

After she was gone, Chance sat back down at the bar and thought about what Paisley had said. When he thought of Everly as a child, he pictured a cute little hellion with a lopsided ponytail and a popsicle-stained mouth competing with the boys at kickball. He did not picture a perfect little angel who played quietly in her room with her dolls.

No wonder she was so bold and outspoken. As a child, she'd been forced to be someone she wasn't. The thought of her being scolded for being the honest person she was made Chance more than a little angry. And not just at Everly's parents. He felt angry with himself.

He hadn't accepted Everly for who she was either. He'd judged her and found her lacking just like her parents. He'd even pushed her to leave town. He'd acted like he was doing it to protect his brother, but deep down, he knew it had more to do with protecting himself.

Everly made him feel. She made him angry and annoyed. Frustrated and exasperated. She made him smile. She made him laugh. She made him face things he didn't want to face.

"Way to go, Preach."

He turned to see Everly coming down the stairs. She did not look happy.

"I give you one job." She held up her finger as she weaved around the tables. "One little job and you blew it. Paisley still refuses to press charges. Which means I'm going to have to head to Mesaville and make sure that sonofabitch regrets what he did myself."

Chance thought she meant in the future until she headed for the door. He jumped up and caught her around the waist.

"Hold on, Everly. This isn't how to go about this."

"I'm not going to turn the other cheek if that's what you want me to do. Now let me go, Preach."

"Not until you calm down." He shifted his hands to tighten his hold and his fingers brushed against the soft, warm skin of her waist. The feelings he'd felt when they'd kissed came flooding back. The heat. The desire. The need. His gaze lowered to her mouth.

"Are you thinking about kissing me, Preach?"

Everly's words worked like a bucket of cold water. Chance released her and stepped back.

"No."

She sent him a sassy smile. "Yes, you were. You were going to kiss me."

"I was not going to kiss you."

She placed a hand on his chest right over his heart that beat out of control and leaned closer until her lips were only a breath away from his. "Liar."

He waited for her to do exactly what she always did—whatever she wanted—and press those full lips against his. Instead, she drew back and sighed.

"Fine. I'll do the Christian thing and won't kick the wife beater's ass. But if he should ever come here, I'm going to make him wish he'd never touched my—"

"What's a wife beater? Is it like an eggbeater?"

Chance turned to see a little boy standing there in dinosaur pajamas. He smiled. "You must be Henry."

The boy nodded. "Henry James Stanford. Henry after my daddy's grandpa who's dead and James after my mama's grandpa who's dead too."

Chance held out his hand. "It's nice to meet you, Henry James Stanford. I'm Chance Wallace Ransom."

"Are you my Aunt Eberly's husband?"

"Absolutely not," Everly said. "Your Aunt

Everly doesn't have a husband. Nor does she want one."

Henry nodded. "That's smart. Sometimes husbands can get bery mean."

Obviously, Henry had seen more than Paisley thought.

A sad look settled on Everly's face. "Yeah, sometimes they can. Now how would you like to go get the best donut you've ever put in your mouth?" She looked at Chance. "You want to treat two hungry Graysons to a donut, Preach?"

# Chapter Eleven

Things were starting to get weird between Everly and Chance.

He'd been about to kiss her. And she'd been about to let him. Now she had invited him for donuts? Of course, that was only because she didn't want to deal with Henry by herself.

The kid scared the hell out of her.

Probably because he was almost as blunt as she was.

"How come you got a heart right there?" Henry poked her in the boob with his little finger. "Hearts are supposed to be on the inside, not the outside."

"Watch what you're touching there, champ," Everly said. "You can't go around poking women in the boobs unless you ask permission."

Henry licked at the donut glaze that surrounded his mouth after he'd inhaled a donut. "My mama says not to use that word. She says to call them breasts."

"And what's so wrong with the word *boob*?"

"Everly," Chance said in the tone he always used when he thought she was crossing a line.

She was about to argue that boob wasn't a bad word when her thoughts just sort of disintegrated in her head at the sight of Chance sitting across from her.

He looked as tempting as the plate of donuts Thelma Davenport had placed in the middle of the table. His sandy hair was mussed and his beard was thicker than she'd ever seen it. It made him look less mild-mannered preacher and more super-hot lumberjack guy. She couldn't help wondering what his beard would feel like sliding along her neck and gently rubbing against the inside of her thighs as he—

She straightened in her chair. What was the matter with her? She was sitting at a table with her four-year-old nephew. She had no business thinking what she'd been thinking. In fact, she had no business thinking what she'd been thinking anywhere. Ever.

"Are you okay?" Chance asked. "You look a little flushed. Are you sure you aren't coming down with something?"

"I'm fine," she said, even though she wasn't sure.

Things had changed between her and Chance after she'd nursed him back to health and she wasn't sure why. Yeah, the Christmas tree kiss had been hot, but she'd kissed great kissers before without lasting effects. And there were definitely lasting effects. When she'd seen him shooting hoops with his brother, her heart had done a crazy little leap in her chest and her lungs suddenly felt like she'd run a marathon.

It had to be the beard.

Although Shane had grown his beard out numerous times and not once had she fantasized about how it would feel between her thighs. In fact, now that she thought about it, her fantasies about Shane had been extremely tame. They had been more about their future than sex. She dreamed about how Shane would run a software company and she would one day own her own restaurant. They'd buy a nice house in Dallas and continue to be the best of friends.

Sex hadn't played a major role in her fantasies.

But now, sex seemed to be all she could think about.

She watched as Chance picked up a donut and took a bite. The way his teeth and lips sank into the glossy glaze and the soft yeasty bread made her heart rate increase and her breath get hung up in her lungs.

"Why do your boobs habe bumps?"

Everly caught Henry's hand right before his finger was about to touch her nipple. Her hard nipple. Chance choked on his donut while Everly glared at her nephew.

"What did I tell you about poking women in the boob without asking permission?"

"Sorry. Can I touch your boob, Aunt Eberly? My mama's boobs don't habe bumps that stick out like that."

"Because your mama wears bras that are thick enough to stop an assassination attempt. While your Aunt Everly doesn't wear—"

"Everly," Chance cut in. "I think that's a little too much information."

"Sorry." She looked back at Henry. "No, you may not touch my boobs." The kid looked totally disappointed and she snorted and shook her head. "Typical man."

Chance laughed. He actually laughed. When she glanced over at him, he had the audacity to shrug. "It's just the way we're made." He looked at Henry. "How would you like to sit up at the counter and watch Otis flip pancakes? It's pretty amazing. He can toss the pancake out of the pan, straight up into the air, and then catch it right back in the pan. On the opposite side."

Henry's eyes were wide. "Nuh-uh."

"Yes, sir. Just sit right over there on that stool and watch."

Henry scrambled out of his chair and headed over to the counter that was decorated with silver tinsel and red bows. After climbing up on a stool, he sat there staring at Otis as if he were a circus performer.

"Way to save my boobs, Preach." She thought she'd get another *Everly*. Instead, he surprised her by laughing again. What was happening? Had she entered an alternate universe without realizing it?

"Henry is certainly a character." Chance cocked an eyebrow at her. "He reminds me of someone else I know."

"I have never gone around poking women in their boobs."

"You would if you wanted to."

She had to concede the point. "Fine. I guess the brat does act a little like his aunt. Which is shocking, considering Paisley is his mother."

Just the mention of Paisley had an image of her sister's battered face popping into her head. Her hands tightened around the coffee mug she'd just picked up. Some of her anger was directed at Paisley's asshole husband. But some was directed at herself. "I should've checked up on Paisley sooner. If I had, I could've stopped the jerk from hurting her."

Chance set his donut down on his plate and picked up his napkin. "You couldn't have stopped it. Paisley probably wouldn't have even told you what was going on."

"I don't get it. Why didn't she leave sooner?"

"Because she kept thinking things would change. It's hard to accept the truth when it's ugly." He paused. "It's been hard for me to accept that Lori is gone. It was hard for you to accept that Shane didn't love you like you loved him."

"Wait a second, did you just say She Who Shall Not Be Named's name? It was the Christmas tree, wasn't it?" She punched the air. "I knew that would pull you out of your funk."

He cleared his throat. "As I was saying, if anyone should understand your sister ignoring the truth, it's you."

"I just ignored Shane not being interested in me as anything but a friend. Paisley ignored getting her face punched in. I think those are two completely different things, Preach."

"Love is blind. It doesn't matter the degree." He hesitated. "But why did you wait so long to contact your sister?"

She shrugged. "I thought she didn't want

anything to do with me. She certainly didn't act like she did. She seemed as annoyed by who I am as my parents are. I think she still might be. I'm just the only person she could turn to."

Chance shook his head. "I don't believe that. When I talked to her, she sounded very proud of who you are. I think she was just too scared to go against your parents. She's not as strong as you, Everly."

His word choice stunned her. "Strong? I'm not strong."

Chance laughed. "You are one of the strongest women I've ever met in my life. And the biggest smart . . .butt."

"Ooo, smartbutt. Is that smartass's little sister?"

"My point exactly." He smiled and a funny flutter took up residence in her stomach. Thinking she was still hungry, she stole the donut from his plate and took a bite.

"What else did my sister say?"

He didn't answer right away. He seemed to be studying her mouth. Once again, her heart seemed to speed up and her breath hitched. He pulled a napkin out of the dispenser and held it out. "You have some icing on your . . ."

"Oh." She took the napkin and wiped her mouth. "Well, don't keep me in suspense, Preach. What did my sister say?"

"Just that she wished she'd stood up for you more when you were kids." He hesitated. "It sounds like you were the odd man out."

"That's putting it mildly. I was the weird duckling in a family of perfect swans."

This time, he didn't laugh. His eyes held compassion. "Or maybe you were the swan in a family of ordinary ducks."

She didn't know why a lump formed at the back of her throat. But she didn't like the feeling. She didn't like it at all. She forced a laugh. "A swan? Not likely. And it doesn't matter. Paisley is my sister and I need to figure out how to help her. She and Henry can't live over a bar. Especially when I filled the spare room with cat toys. Although Henry seems to love squeezing into the cat condo and pretending he's a cat. Still, the room is right over the jukebox and my sister has trouble getting Henry to sleep with the music coming through the floor."

Chance reclaimed the donut she'd set down. It seemed they were now sharing donuts. "What about the Kingman Ranch? I'm sure they'll have room for your sister and Henry."

She shook her head. "I already thought about that, but Paisley doesn't want anyone to see her until her face heals."

"We could see if the Malones would rent your sister their spare room. It has a separate entrance and she could stay with you at the bar until it opens and then go back to the Malones' at night."

"We?"

He cleared his throat. "As you pointed out, it's pretty much my job to take care of people in need. I'll talk to Hester today."

She wanted to say she could handle it. But after her and Hester's last conversation, Everly had no desire to talk to the fortune-teller. If the woman found out Everly had nursed Chance back to health, she would no doubt think her prediction of Everly being Chance's savior had come true.

Weirdly, it had.

Everly *had* come to Chance's rescue when he'd been sick, but only because no one else seemed to be willing to. And putting up the Christmas tree *had* seemed to help with his grieving process.

"You want the last bite?" Chance held out the donut.

She should decline. She really should. But before she could stop herself, she leaned over and took the donut from his fingers. It tasted both sweet and salty. Or maybe it was the skin her tongue brushed over that tasted salty. Either way, it was the best bite of donut she'd ever had in her life.

Rather than looking shocked, Chance just stared at her with steamy coffee eyes as she drew her lips across his fingers. Even after she sat back in her chair, his hand remained suspended in midair.

She wanted to say something snarky to break the sizzling tension, but for once in her life, she had nothing. She didn't know how long she sat there with her gaze locked with Chance's and the taste of his skin mingling with the sugary bite of donut in her mouth.

It took the bell on the door jangling to startle them out of their trances.

Kitty Carson came hustling in with her huge mailbag slung over her shoulder. She headed toward Thelma, who was busy hanging more

Christmas tinsel along the register counter, but Kitty stopped short when she saw Everly and Chance. Her buckteeth flashed in a smile.

"Well, hey, y'all! It's good to see you out and about, Reverend Ransom. Did you try those salted caramel brownies I left in your mailbox? My mama made them and, while she can completely ruin a box of Kraft mac and cheese, she's got a way with anything to do with chocolate and sugar."

Chance got to his feet and smiled at Kitty. "I did try them. Tell your mother they were delicious."

"Will do." Kitty looked at Everly. "And how are you doing, Cowboy Scrooge? You ready to put those pipes of yours to work?"

Everly figured it was time to set Kitty straight. "I'm sorry, Kitty, but—"

"Cowboy Scooge?" Henry climbed onto the chair next to Everly. "What's a Cowboy Scooge, Aunt Eberly?"

"Now who is this sweet little cowboy?" Kitty asked.

"This is my nephew, Henry," Everly said. "He and my sister are visiting for a few weeks. Now about the Christmas mus—"

"Well, isn't that a nice surprise. Nothing like being with kids around the holidays." Kitty glanced at Chance. "You like kids, don't you, Reverend?"

Chance seemed taken back by the question that had come out of nowhere. "Umm . . . yes."

Kitty's smile got even bigger. "That's good. That's real good." Her gaze shot back to Everly.

"Nothing like a man who loves kids, right, Everly?" At a complete loss of what was going on, Everly just stared at her.

Kitty plopped her mailbag on the empty chair and held out a hand to Henry. "Hi, Henry. I'm Kitty Carson. And it just so happens that I have something special for visiting nephews." She pulled a red envelope with a border of candy canes out of her mailbag and handed it to Henry. "This here is addressed to Santa Claus himself. Inside, you'll find a blank sheet of paper to write the jolly ol' elf a letter telling him exactly what you want for Christmas. Then you'll give it back to me and I'll make sure it gets to the North Pole. As for your question, Cowboy Scrooge is only the meanest sidewinder this side of the Pecos."

Henry stared at her. "What's a sidewinder?"

"It's a lowdown snake."

Henry's eyes widened. "A snake? Are you calling my Aunt Eberly a lowdown snake?"

"No, sirree. I would never do that. Cowboy Scrooge is just a character that your aunt's going to play in our Christmas show. And Reverend Ransom here is going to direct it."

"About that," Everly said. "I'm not—"

"I want to be a cowboy snake in a Christmas show!" Henry yelled at the top of his lungs. "I want to be a cowboy snake!"

"Oh, no," Everly said. "You aren't going to be in the play." Suddenly, out of nowhere, Henry fell onto the floor and started throwing a fit to beat all fits.

"I want to be a sidewinder! I want to be a sidewinder!"

While Everly tried to figure out how to deal with her nephew's temper tantrum, Kitty looked at Chance and smiled. "'Ask and you shall receive', Reverend. Looks like we got our Scrooge and our Tiny Wrangler Tim."

# Chapter Twelve

CHRISTMAS HAD COME to Cursed, Texas, overnight.

As Chance drove his truck down the main street, he felt like he was driving through a Hallmark movie set. Every store window was lined with twinkle lights and had a glittering Christmas tree. Or two. The Cursed Seed and Feed had two trees both heavily decorated with horseshoes, cowbells, and loops of lassoes. The big spruce in front of the post office had been covered in bows and shiny red balls. Every streetlight had either a cowboy snowman or a cowboy Santa waving from it. And the Malones' house had more lights on it than Clark Griswold's.

It looked like Hester was busy putting up even more. She stood on a tall ladder stapling twinkle lights under the eaves of the porch. Which didn't seem like a good idea given how windy it was.

Chance quickly parked his truck and hurried over to help. "Let me do that for you, Hester."

Hester only gave him a glance before she finished stapling the end of the string of lights. "Thanks, but I got it." She checked to see if the lights were secure before she started down the ladder. At the bottom, she turned to Chance and smiled. "What brings you here today, Reverend? Do you need a haircut or a palm reading? Or both?"

"I probably could use a haircut, but I stopped by to see if your rental room was available for the next few weeks."

"Are you having out-of-town guests for the holidays?"

"Not me, but Everly. Her sister and nephew are visiting and Nasty Jack's is a little too rowdy at night for a four-year-old to sleep."

Hester nodded. "I heard about Everly's sister and nephew visiting. Kitty is thrilled that we not only have a Cowboy Scrooge, but also an enthusiastic Tiny Wrangler Tim."

Chance couldn't help but smile at the thought of Everly caving to her nephew's tears and agreeing to be Scrooge so Henry could be in the play. Of course, Chance had caved too about canceling the play. He couldn't bring himself to disappoint a little boy who had already been through so much.

"I believe he wants to be called Tiny Sidewinder Tim," he said.

Hester laughed. "It sounds like Everly's nephew is a pip."

"That's putting it mildly. He acts just like his aunt."

"Nothing wrong with that. Everly is the type of woman who doesn't have a problem going after what she wants." Hester hesitated. "Even if what she wants is all wrong for her."

Chance didn't know why he suddenly felt defensive. It certainly wasn't his place to defend Everly. And yet, he did. "I don't think she's still going after Shane, if that's what you're alluding to."

"And how do you know that?"

It was a good question. One he didn't have a good answer for. "Just a gut feeling."

Hester nodded. "Never underestimate gut feelings. Your gut is usually right. And I agree. Everly is over Shane." Her intense gaze settled on him. "So it appears that you and Everly have become friends. Especially if you're here asking about a room for her sister."

Chance had accepted that he and Everly were friends . . . who had kissed numerous times. He tried not to make too much of the kisses. It had been a long time since he'd been with a woman and Everly was an extremely attractive woman. It made sense that he would feel desire for her. He just didn't plan on giving in to that desire. What he did plan on doing was helping her with her sister and Henry as much as he could. It was the least he could do after Everly had taken care of him while he was sick.

"Everly's pretty busy with her job, the kittens, and now her sister and nephew," he said. "So I volunteered to ask you about the rental room."

Hester nodded. "That's what friends are for. To lend a hand when you're struggling to keep your head above water. And I would love to help Everly's sister out. Unfortunately, the basement room is already rented for the next two weeks. But I'd be happy to offer her and her son the two spare rooms in my house. I thought my daughter was coming for Christmas, but Aurora now has plans to go to Scotland for some mystical seminar."

"I'm sorry your daughter can't come, but I'm sure Paisley will appreciate the offer." While it wasn't his place to go into detail, he figured Hester did need a little information. "Paisley's been through a lot and can use a little help." He pulled out his wallet. "In fact, I'd like to pay for the rooms."

Hester held up her hand. "I'm not taking money from a preacher. Or a young woman who needs some help. Especially when Everly was the one who came up with the idea to have a house raising to rebuild our house and Mystic's business after the tornado."

"Thank you." Chance slipped his wallet back in his pocket. "And speaking of Mystic, I hear you're going to be a great-grandmother. Congratulations."

Hester beamed. "It is exciting news. I'm looking forward to teaching a new Malone all my tricks." She winked. "Now why don't you come inside, Reverend Ransom, and I'll make us a cup of tea and check to see if Mystic has an opening to give you a haircut."

Chance hadn't been inside the house since Hester had moved back in. It was obvious a psychic lived there. A crystal ball sat on a table in one corner. And a small potted Christmas tree covered in crystals and hand-blown glass balls sat by the fireplace and caught the sunlight coming in through the window, refracting it around the room. In the kitchen, tarot cards were spread out on the table.

As Hester collected the cards, Wish appeared and rubbed against Chance's legs. He leaned over to pet the cat. "Hey, Wish, you remember me? You stayed the night with me after the tornado. Or not me as much as Everly. She was the one who found you."

"I heard you gave them both shelter from the storm," Hester said.

Everly had been renting the Malones' basement room when the tornado hit. Thankfully, she had been at the bar and hadn't gotten hurt. Once the tornado had passed, she found Wish and brought the cat to the parsonage. They had spent the night in his guest room. But, looking back, he hadn't been very hospitable. He had still been leery of her motives for coming to Cursed.

He straightened. "I didn't do nearly as much as I should have."

"I doubt Everly would've let you do much. The ladies of the Auxiliary Club tried to give her clothes and toiletries, but she had already gone into Amarillo and gotten what she needed."

"Of course she did. Everly doesn't need anyone's help."

Hester slid the tarot cards into their case. "Or so she tries to make everyone think. How are the kittens? Does she still think she's going to be able to give them away?"

"Yes. She's too stubborn to admit she's fallen in love with them."

Hester moved to the stove and picked up the teakettle. "She'll figure it out eventually. Sometimes it takes a while for us to realize what we need in our lives to make us happy. Sit down, Reverend. It will just take me a minute to make the tea."

There was something soothing about watching Hester make tea. Her full skirts swayed as she filled the kettle with filtered water from a large bottle and put it on the burner. Then she opened a can of tea and filled a strainer with the loose leaves before placing it on a teapot. When the kettle whistled, she poured the hot water over the leaves, then set a tray with cups, a sugar container, spoons, and a plate of homemade ginger snap cookies.

Once again, he was reminded of his Granny Ran. She had loved making cookies and ginger snaps had been her favorite. He could remember her singing hymns as she baked in the tiny little trailer kitchen. She had lost so much. Her parents, her husband, her son. But she had never lost her faith. She had never quit. If she had, Shane and Chance would have ended up in a foster home and their lives would have been a lot different. Instead, Granny Ran had taken them in and put up with two little boys who had been as rowdy as Henry.

The thought of Granny Ran's sacrifices made

Chance feel extremely guilty for giving up so easily after Lori had passed away. His grandmother had taught him better.

"Grandmothers are a gift."

Chance glanced over to find Hester watching him. "How did you know I was thinking of my grandmother?"

She placed the teapot on the tray and carried it over to the table. "You had the kind of smile people get when they're reminiscing. And since you told me your grandmother raised you, it was a lucky guess." She sat down and poured the tea into the cups and then handed him one. "So tell me about her."

He had lumped his grandmother's passing with Lori's and hadn't really grieved her properly. It seemed right that he would do so now with a woman who reminded him so much of Granny Ran. As he sipped the dark-flavored tea and ate the spicy ginger snaps, he told Hester about his life growing up in his grandmother's tiny little trailer. About how Granny Ran had taken him and Shane in after their father and mother had been too addicted to drugs to care for them. How she had raised them to be strong, faithful, kind men who knew the value of hard work.

"She sounds like a good woman," Hester said. "You and Shane were lucky to have her. And she was lucky to have you."

"I don't know about that." Chance finished off his third cookie. "I was a handful."

"Handful or not. Grandkids are blessings. I'm sure your grandmother felt blessed to have you and Shane. Just like I feel blessed to have Mystic."

Chance wiped his mouth with a napkin. "I hope so. Although if she could see me now, I'd get a stern lecture. She believed that happiness wasn't something you were given. It was something you had to work for. I haven't worked very hard at it lately."

Hester's piercing gaze settled on him. "So you aren't happy?"

At one time, his answer would have been a resounding no. With no small amount of surprise, he realized that was no longer true. He wasn't happy, but he wasn't unhappy either. He was somewhere in between. He didn't jump up in the morning looking forward to the day. Nor did he lie in bed dreading getting up and facing it.

"I'm not as sad as I was." He wasn't answering Hester as much as just confirming the truth to himself . . . letting it seep in and give him something he hadn't had in a long time.

Hope.

"So does that mean you're not quitting as pastor?" Hester asked.

He wasn't surprised she knew. "I guess Shane told you."

"No one told me. I got the feeling when the church board interviewed you that you didn't really want the job. Am I wrong?"

He shook his head. "You're not wrong. I plan to resign after the first of the year. But I would appreciate you keeping that between us."

"I don't divulge what people tell me." She poured them each another cup of tea, then stirred sugar into hers, first one way and then the other, before placing the spoon on the table next to her cup. "Why do you think you're not as sad as you once were, Chance?"

It was the first time she'd called him by his given name. Again he was reminded of his grandmother. Granny Ran always said his and Shane's names in a certain tone when she wanted them to really think about what she was asking.

So he gave Hester's question some thought. What *had* caused his grieving to lessen? One image popped into his head. An image of a fiery-haired woman with whiskey eyes and a smart mouth . . . and soft, irresistible lips.

But that's not what he said. "Time, I guess."

Hester arched her brows. While her hair was silver, her eyebrows were jet black. The contrast was dramatic. "Time? So you're one of those people who believe that time heals all wounds?"

"You don't?"

"No. I believe that love heals all wounds. And all of the people who love you are right here in Cursed. It would be foolish to leave what's healing you."

The woman made sense, but there was another reason for resigning. "I'm no longer the right man for the job."

She tipped her head. "Because you're struggling with your faith?"

Again, he wasn't surprised. Hester was the one who had told Shane that Chance had lost his faith. How she had figured it out, he wasn't sure. Maybe she was a psychic. Or just intuitive like

Granny Ran. Either way, he didn't try to deny it.

"A faithless pastor is the last thing this town needs."

She studied him. "But maybe Cursed is exactly what a faithless pastor needs."

While he was absorbing Hester's words, the front door opened and Kitty Carson's voice rang out. "Hey, Witchy Woman! I'm here for my afternoon tea and to discuss our matchmaking pla—" She cut off when she stepped into the kitchen and saw Chance. "Well, hey, Reverend Ransom. I didn't realize you were here."

Chance stood and pushed in his chair. "I was just leaving. I don't want to interrupt your afternoon tea." He winked. "Or your matchmaking plans."

Kitty smiled weakly. "Heard that, did you? Hester and I are trying to get . . . Sam Eckhart and Debbie Schumer together."

Chance stared at her with surprise. "Sam and Debbie? Aren't they both in their nineties?"

"Love has no age limits, Reverend. Why, I wouldn't be surprised if we don't have ourselves a Christmas weddin'." She glanced at Hester. "Ain't that right, Witchy Woman?"

Hester rolled her eyes. "Only if you can learn to keep your mouth shut. Which I'm beginning to believe is an impossibility."

# Chapter Thirteen

"Are you going to take my hand, Aunt Eberly? Mama always says I need to hold hands in a parking lot."

Everly looked down at Henry, who hadn't stopped talking since he'd arrived in Cursed. For the last couple days, the kid had done nothing but follow her around and chatter. She knew it had to be hard on him to be jerked from his home with everything that was familiar and taken to a strange place with a strange woman he didn't know. She was trying her best to be patient and understanding. But her patience had about run out. Especially since he was the reason she was at the church musical rehearsal in the first place. And a good thirty minutes too early. He had bugged her nonstop about being late for rehearsal until she had finally buckled him into his booster seat and brought him to church.

"Are you mad at me, Aunt Eberly?"

She pulled out of her thoughts to see Henry staring up at her with big teary eyes. The kid could break her heart with just one look. She took his hand in hers and gave it a reassuring squeeze before she led him toward the church.

"No, I'm not mad at you, Henry. But I am a little annoyed with you for throwing a big fit and getting me stuck doing a stupid church musical. And it's not Eberly. It's Everly with a *v*. Evvv-erly."

"Ebbb-erly." She rolled her eyes as he continued to jabber. "And how come you don't want to be Cowboy Scooge, Aunt Eberly? I bet you'll get to wear a cowboy hat and boots. Will I get to wear a cowboy hat and boots with my snake costume?" She had told Henry a thousand times Kitty hadn't been talking about an actual snake when she'd said he could be a sidewinder, but he refused to listen. Just like he wasn't listening now. "I can't be a sidewinder without a cowboy hat and boots. I had a pair of boots, but Mama forgot to pack them. She also forgot my Spider-Man pajamas and my fuzzy blanket and my *PAW Patrol* toothbrush and my light-up tennis shoes and my T. rex and my stuffed shark and my—"

Everly cut in before Henry could go through the entire list. A list she'd already heard over and over again. "I get it. She forgot to pack a lot of your favorite things. But didn't I buy you some cool stuff today at the Walmart in Amarillo?"

"Not cowboy boots. Or light-up tennis shoes or a stuffed shark or a—"

"Enough already." She held open the church door for him. "I know I didn't get you everything you wanted. But you don't get everything you want in life. Sometimes you get what you get and you don't throw a fit."

His bottom lip started to tremble as they stepped into the church foyer. "Does that mean I don't get a cowboy hat and boots?"

Before she could pull all her hair out and go screaming into the streets, she noticed Chance and the skinny woman who played the organ standing in the foyer. Although she barely noticed the woman. Her eyes were pinned on Chance.

Tonight, he wore blue jeans and a white western shirt with the cuffs folded back on his muscled forearms. He'd trimmed his beard, but he'd left a layer of sexy scruff. It looked like he'd gotten a haircut, but he hadn't slicked it back like he usually did. Instead, his hair fell over his forehead and the tops of his ears in dark wheat-colored waves that she had the sudden urge to run her fingers through.

Everly's heart did the crazy little skip thing.

Suddenly, she realized that her frustration had nothing to do with her talkative nephew or being stuck playing Cowboy Scrooge in a small-town musical. Her frustration had to do with herself and her body's reaction to the man looking back at her with twinkling coffee eyes.

She was not falling for another Ransom.

She was NOT!

"Pastor Chance!" Henry ran over and hugged Chance's legs—legs that looked awfully good in the faded blue jeans. *Stop it, Everly. Stop it, right now!* "Guess what?" Henry hollered loud enough for the people in the next county to hear. "Aunt Eberly said I don't get a cowboy hat and boots to go with my snake costume."

Chance glanced at Everly. "A snake costume?"

Not wanting to go into a long, drawn-out explanation, Everly just shrugged. "Yeah, he wants a snake costume."

Chance nodded. "I'll talk to Hester and see what she can do. In the meantime . . ." He plopped the Stetson he was holding on Henry's head. "You can wear my hat." The kid beamed as if he'd just been given a solid gold crown.

"Thanks, Pastor Chance."

"Anytime, buddy." Chance placed a hand on Henry's shoulder. Something about the large hand resting on her nephew's small shoulder caused the weird thing to happen to her heart again. Maybe she needed to go to the doctor's. Maybe she had a heart condition.

"There's someone I'd like you and your aunt to meet, Henry." Chance cut into her thoughts. "This is Diana Moody. Mrs. Moody, this is Everly Grayson and Henry Stanford."

"Henry James Stanford." Henry corrected him. "And guess what? My aunt has my same middle name too. Eberly James."

Chance glanced at Everly and smiled. And damned if her breath didn't catch. "Mrs. Moody, I'd like you to meet Henry James Stanford and Everly James Grayson. Mrs. Moody is going to be the Ghost of Christmas Past."

Henry's eyes got huge. "A ghost? You're a ghost?"

Mrs. Moody laughed. "Only in the play. I'm also going to help you and the other children learn your lines and songs." She leaned down to Henry and whispered. "And I brought candy canes to hand out to the good listeners."

"I'll listen!" Henry yelled at the top of his lungs. "I'll be the best listening snake this side of the Pecos." He cocked his head, causing Chance's hat to shift. "Do snakes have ears?"

"That's a good question, Henry." Mrs. Moody took his hand. "Snakes don't have external ears, but they do have all the parts of the inner ear we do. I happen to have a book on snakes I'll be happy to loan you. But for now, you can come upstairs with me to the Sunday school room and help me get everything ready for when the other children arrive."

With an excited look on his face, Henry followed her up the stairs that led to the second story. Halfway up, he came to a dead stop and turned back to Everly. "You'll be right here when I'm done, won't you, Aunt Eberly?"

No matter how big of a chatterbox he'd been the last few days, there had been moments—like this one—when he'd made Everly's heart squeeze. "Of course, I'll be here. As your aunt, we're stuck with each other."

"Like glue?"

Everly nodded. "Superglue."

Henry's smile returned and he let Mrs. Moody lead him up the stairs.

When they were gone, Everly blew out her breath.

"Hard day?" Chance asked.

"I swear the kid can suck the energy right out of you like he sucks the juice out of those little boxes he can't seem to get enough of." When Chance laughed, she glared at him. "You think it's funny, do you? I'd like to see you spend three days with a four-year-old who won't give you a moment's peace. And Paisley can't help because she's barely getting up in the mornings." She paused. "Thanks for coming by to talk to her every day. It seems to be the only thing that gets her out of bed and dressed."

"She has a lot to deal with. It's nice she has a sister who is willing to watch Henry while she's getting through it. It's also nice that you agreed to be Cowboy Scrooge so Henry could be . . . a snake." Again he smiled. He was doing a lot of smiling this evening and it was freaking her out. Where was the man who walked around with a perpetual frown on his face?

"Okay, what's going on with you?" she asked. "I thought you were hoping that I wouldn't be Cowboy Scrooge so you could cancel the play. And now you're all smiley and happy about directing the musical. Your mood swings are scaring me, Preach."

He sent her a skeptical look. "I doubt anything scares you, Everly."

"Then you would be wrong. Clowns scare the hell out of me." She glanced up and offered a silent apology to God for cussing in his house. "And spiders and bees scare me. Carnies, jack-in-the-boxes, gray hairs, cockroaches, warts, four-year-old kids, and grumpy preachers who suddenly start smiling." She leaned closer. "You can tell me. I'm great at keeping secrets. Did you sell your soul to the devil and are now just a robot doing Satan's will?"

He laughed. It completely transformed his face. How did the man get better looking every time she saw him? She had thought he and Shane were identical twins, but now she knew all their differences. From their smiles to their eye color to the way their hair fell over their foreheads.

"Checking for gray hairs, Everly? Or maybe a robot battery?"

Realizing she'd been caught staring, she pulled her gaze away from his hair and shrugged. "I'm just waiting for an answer, Preach. What's going on with you?"

"Maybe I just have the Christmas spirit. And speaking of Christmas." He pulled a folded script from his back pocket and handed it to her. "I thought you might want to go over this before everyone gets here. I need to talk with Mr. Olson about getting a Christmas tree for the foyer before he leaves for the night."

Her eyes widened. He wanted to put up a Christmas tree? Something was going on with him. But before she could start interrogating him again, he turned and walked away. With nothing else to do, she took the script into the chapel and sat in the front pew.

With the title, she had expected the musical to be hokey. But it wasn't hokey as much as clever. It followed the same storyline as *A Christmas*

*Carol*, but with a country flair that was hilarious. Scrooge was a grumpy rancher who hid away in his castle—a castle that sounded suspiciously like the Kingmans' home—and made everyone's life miserable. Especially his ranch hand, Billy Bob Cratchit. Everly was laughing over a particularly funny line Billy Bob said to Cowboy Scrooge when Chance showed back up.

"I guess it's pretty bad."

She glanced up at him. "You didn't read it?"

"I heard parts of it during auditions, but I haven't read the entire play."

"You're the director and you didn't even read the script?" She mimicked Kitty Carson and shook her head. "Just a cryin' shame, Preach. Just a cryin' shame."

"Hey, I've been a little busy lately."

Since he'd been a little busy helping her sister, she didn't continue to tease him. "It's not that bad. I mean some of the songs are a little silly, but cute." She flipped back a few pages. "Like this one." She started to sing, but then realized it would be so much better with music. She stood and headed up the steps of the stage to the grand piano.

It had been a while since she played, but as soon as her fingers touched the keys, it all came back to her. When she had the melody down, she started singing the lyrics about a lowdown, grumpy sidewinder who held an entire small town in his greedy clutches.

As she sang and played, she realized just how much she'd missed playing the piano. Growing up, it had always been something she'd been forced to do—a job to show off her skills to other people rather than a pleasure. It didn't feel like that tonight.

It felt like a . . . gift.

Which was silly. She wasn't gifted by any means.

This was confirmed when she glanced at Chance and saw his stunned face.

She stopped playing. "Okay, so I'm a bit rusty. I was just trying to prove to you that the musical isn't as bad as we both thought."

He continued to stare at her. "That was amazing."

She couldn't help the blush that heated her cheeks. She forced a laugh to cover her embarrassment. "I thought preachers weren't supposed to lie."

"It wasn't a lie, Everly. Whoever told you that you weren't good was the liar."

"Hey, don't call my parents liars, Preach."

She meant it as a joke, but Chance didn't laugh. He studied her for a long moment before he spoke. "I think I'm starting to understand. Like all children, you hated disappointing your parents. Which is why you try to set everyone else's expectations of you so low. You don't want to disappoint them too."

Whoever said the truth hurts wasn't lying. Looking at yourself through someone else's objective lens was hard to take. Everly certainly couldn't take it.

"Don't try to psychoanalyze me, Preach. That's a deep, dark hole you don't want to go down."

"I'm not trying to psychoanalyze you. I'm just making an observation." He arched a brow. "Something you've done a time or two with me."

"Well, stop. My sister needs your help, I don't."

He nodded. "Okay. But I hope you know that your parents' disappointment wasn't in you, Everly. It was in themselves. They took their own insecurities out on you and Paisley because they didn't know how else to deal with them."

Deep down, she had always known that. But for some reason, it held so much more power when someone else confirmed it. Or maybe not someone. Chance. He wasn't the kind of man who randomly said things without giving them a lot of thought. He believed in the words he spoke. Which is why his next words stunned her so much.

"You're a talented, strong, kind woman, Everly. Any parent should be proud to have you as a daughter. If yours aren't, that's their problem, not yours."

A burning sensation pressed against the back of her eyes, and she couldn't hold back the tears that welled into them. She quickly looked away and started flipping through the pages of the script in hopes Chance hadn't noticed. But a moment later, a tissue appeared in front of her face. Before she could think of something snarky to say, he spoke.

"For your allergies. I guess I need to talk to Mr. Olson about cleaning out the air ducts."

She blinked the tears away before she turned to him. "Are you sure you haven't sold your soul to the devil, Preach? You sure are acting weird. Smiling all the time, handing out compliments, acting like you actually like me."

He hesitated for a moment before he answered. "I didn't sell my soul. I think I found it."

## Chapter Fourteen

"DID YOU BRING an ax to chop down our Christmas tree, Pastor Chance? Or a chainsaw? I hope it's a chainsaw, 'cause I never habe used a chainsaw before. And a chainsaw would cut right through anything. I bet it could eben cut through a steel building if it was big enough. How big is your chainsaw? Could it cut through a steel building?"

Chance glanced in the rearview mirror at Henry, who was sitting in his booster seat looking like he could burst from excitement.

Chance hadn't planned on a tree-cutting excursion. He'd planned to give Mr. Olson money to get a tree for the church at a lot in Amarillo. But when Buck had picked up Mystic from rehearsal and found out about Chance needing a tree, he'd offered a tree from the Kingman Ranch—if Chance was willing to drive out and cut it down. Everly and Henry happened to be standing there at the time. The little boy got so excited about chopping down a tree that Chance couldn't refuse the offer.

As he drove down the dirt road to the Kingman Ranch, he was glad he hadn't.

Henry wasn't the only one excited about chopping down a tree. Chance had never cut his own Christmas tree before either. He'd spent hours at the hardware store looking at axes and saws before deciding on a bow saw with a comfortable handle.

"Sorry, Henry, but I didn't bring a chainsaw. I brought a bow saw because I figured it was something your mother might be okay with you trying. I doubt she'll let you use a chainsaw."

Henry turned to Paisley who sat in the back seat next to him. "Can I, Mama? Can I use Pastor Chance's saw? Please! Plea—"

Everly, who sat in the passenger's seat next to Chance, cut in. "Oh, no. Don't you dare start another fit. If you do, I'm having Chance turn right around and take us back to Cursed."

Chance glanced in the rearview mirror and saw Henry's bottom lip puff out. "You're mean, Aunt Eberly."

"Your aunt isn't mean," Paisley said. "She's right. I've been letting you get away with way too much and you've started to get a little bratty."

Everly turned around to look at her sister. "A little? The kid throws the biggest—"

"Everly," Chance said. "I think Paisley can handle this."

She narrowed her eyes at him, but turned back around.

"So can I chop down the tree, Mama?" Henry asked. "Can I?"

"You can help if Pastor Chance is right there supervising," Paisley said.

"What's super bicing?"

"It means being the one in charge."

"Like Pastor Chance is in charge of the play?" He didn't wait for his mother to answer before he continued. "And guess what, Hessy is making me a snake suit. She measured me all up this morning. She says I'm going to make the best sidewinder she eber saw. And you know what else? She let me look into her magic ball—I couldn't touch it, but I got to look into it. You know what I saw? I saw me with really big eyes and a funny nose. But you know what Hessy saw when she looked into it? She saw me being a cowboy. I bet that was because of my new boots and hat that Pastor Chance got me. Thanks again, Pastor Chance. They are the most awesomest hat and boots eber!" He kicked the back of Chance's seat, no doubt admiring his new boots. "And you know what else . . ."

Henry continued to talk the rest of the way to the Kingman Ranch. He only stopped when the castle came into view. "What's that?"

"That's Buckinghorse Palace," Chance said.

"But it looks like a castle?"

"That's what a palace is," Paisley said. "But I've never seen one on a ranch before."

"Can we go inside? I want to see a palace! I want to see a palace!"

Paisley reached up and touched Everly's shoulder. Whatever telepathic message she sent, Everly received it. "Not today, Henry," Everly said.

"We'll visit the Kingman castle another time."

Chance figured he knew what the message had been. Paisley's face was healing, but the bruises were still obvious and she didn't want anyone to see them. She wore her sunglasses whenever she walked between the Malones' house and Nasty Jack's. She probably even wore them around Hester. Not that Hester wouldn't have already figured things out.

"We're going to drive right by it," Chance said. "So you can get a good look. Then one day soon, if your mother says it's okay, I'll bring you out here and not only show you the castle, but also the stables with the horses."

"Horses?! They got horses? Can I ride one? Can I ride one? 'Cause if I'm gonna be a cowboy—"

"Oh, Lord, here we go again." Everly covered her eyes with her hand and Chance figured she'd had all she could take and cut in.

"How about if we sing some Christmas songs to get us in the tree-cutting mood? Do you know 'Jingle Bells,' Henry?"

Henry started singing "Jingle Bells" and Chance joined in. He didn't know who was the most off-key. When they finished, Everly glanced back at Paisley.

"Should we show these boys how a Christmas carol is done, Paise?"

Chance was surprised that the carol she chose was "Silent Night"—his favorite. Her sister joined in with perfect harmony. Paisley had a beautiful voice, but it didn't affect him like Everly's voice did. Her strong, clear voice touched something deep inside of him. Something he thought he had lost forever.

The will to live.

As much as he hadn't wanted to live after Lori died, the last few weeks had made him realize that he did. He wanted to live and laugh . . . and love again.

He glanced over at Everly.

Her eyes were closed and her chin was lifted. She sang like she did everything in life. With her entire heart. She had a huge one. Something he hadn't seen at first. But he saw it now. She might talk tough, but her actions spoke louder than her words. All her actions, from caring for the three kittens to caring for her sister and nephew, spoke of a big heart. And maybe it wasn't her voice that had pulled him from his self-pitying abyss. Maybe it was the heart she put into her singing and in everything she did.

He had thought the worst thing that could happen was her coming to live in Cursed. But if she hadn't shown up, Chance would have quit preaching by now and be living in some depressing apartment in Dallas still searching for hope. Now he had hope. That's what Everly had given him. Hope that he could find happiness again. He certainly felt happy today.

He joined in on the last verse of "Silent Night," uncaring that he didn't sound half as good as the Grayson sisters. He just wanted to sing.

The section of the ranch Buck had given him directions to was located about five minutes from the house. Buck had told Chance that his grandfather had planted the trees so he'd always have a Christmas tree big enough for his castle. There *were* some huge pines growing. There were also some medium-sized and smaller trees.

Of course, as soon as Henry was out of the truck, he raced toward the biggest row of trees and started yelling, "Theses ones! Theses ones!"

Chance laughed as he reached into the bed of the truck for the bow saw. "Who wants to explain to him that not one of those trees will fit in the church foyer unless we cut a hole in the roof?"

Paisley sighed. "It's best to let him run off some of his energy before we explain anything. I'll keep an eye on him while you two find the tree for the church." She headed after her son while Chance and Everly headed toward the rows of medium-sized trees.

"What in the world were you thinking inviting us along on your tree-hunting expedition, Preach? It would've been a lot easier if you didn't have a chatterbox four-year-old to deal with." Everly shivered and rubbed at her arms as they moved between the rows of trees. The wind had picked up since they'd left Cursed and she wore one of her skimpy tank tops.

Chance stopped and handed her the saw. Her eyebrows lifted. "So that's why you brought us? You expect the Graysons to do all the work?"

He smiled as he shrugged out of his lined jean jacket. "Don't act like you don't want to chop down a tree." He held out his jacket for her. She didn't waste any time slipping her arms in. Once she had it on, he took the saw from her. "You're just as excited as Henry."

She shook her head. "No one can be that excited. Although the kid gets excited over everything. You should've seen him yesterday morning when Otis let him flip a pancake."

"Paisley mentioned you take him to Good Eats every morning." He cocked an eyebrow. "Wouldn't it be more enjoyable to have coffee without a chatterbox four-year-old? I think you like hanging out with Henry as much as I do . . . Aunt Eberly."

Her eyes narrowed. "Watch it, Preach. There's only one person who gets to call me that and he's a pint-sized cutie who struggles with his *v*'s." Her gaze ran over his face. "Although you're lookin' pretty darn cute now that you don't mousse your hair back like some uptight banker and have a little scruff working. Or maybe cute isn't the word. Maybe hot is."

The compliment left him speechless. Thankfully, Everly didn't expect him to reply. She just winked and turned her attention to the trees. "So how tall are you thinking, Preach?"

Everly asked him about the height of the tree, but she didn't want him picking it out. Every time he chose one, she vetoed it for being too scrawny or having bare spots. When he finally found one that met all her requirements, she crawled beneath it to make sure it had a straight trunk.

"What does a straight trunk have to do with anything?" Chance asked as he looked down at

Everly's legs and red cowboy boots sticking out from the low branches. The woman had some great legs. "Once it's decorated, no one will see the trunk."

The branches muffled her voice. "If the trunk isn't straight, the tree will tip over. My father always made sure our trees had straight trunks. Of course, everything had to be straight in our house."

"Which is why you decided to be so kinky." Chance froze when he realized how that had sounded. Before he could correct his blooper, Everly slid out from beneath the tree and stared up at him.

"Did you just call me kinky, Preach?"

"I didn't mean it like it sounded."

She laughed. "You're blushing. Don't tell me you haven't ever gotten a little kinky in the bedroom."

"Everly."

"Don't you *Everly* me. You brought it up. So curious minds want to know." She held out her hand and he pulled her to her feet. Her hair was mussed and littered with pine needles and her amber eyes twinkled mischievously. "Come on, Preach. I'll tell you my kinkiest story if you tell me yours. I'm sure you did something naughty before you became a holier-than-thou preacher. Playacting? Bondage? Maybe a threesome with two wild college girls?"

His face grew even warmer. "There were no college girls. Wild or otherwise."

"High school girls?"

He shook his head.

Her eyes narrowed. "Don't tell me that Lori was your first and only." When he didn't reply, she blinked. "Well, that's just plain pathetic, Preach."

It was such an Everly thing to say that he couldn't help laughing. "I guess some people might think so." He lifted his hand and started picking the needles from her hair.

"So you're telling me that you didn't meet one girl you wanted to go to bed with before Lori?"

"I had desires." He had a desire right now to run his hands through her hair to see how the fiery strands felt slipping through his fingers. Instead, he continued to pluck pine needles. "But I wanted my first time to be with someone I loved."

She stared back at him. In the sunlight, her eyes looked even more golden. Like twin suns spreading warmth to everything they touched. "Okay, that's pretty sweet. But what about now?"

"Now?"

She nodded. "Since I get the feeling you won't ever love anyone like you loved Lori, does that mean you're going to spend the rest of your life without sex?"

It was a good question. One he hadn't given much thought to. "I don't know."

"Then maybe you need to figure it out. I suggest you kiss some girls and see if they get your motor running."

He knew it wasn't an invitation. If Everly wanted to kiss him, she would kiss him. She always did what she felt like doing . . . while he rarely did. Just this once, he wanted to do what he felt like without worrying about what was right and what was wrong.

He stopped pulling out needles and buried his fingers into the fiery tresses. As Everly's eyes widened, he leaned down . . . and kissed the girl.

Her lips were as soft and sweet as he remembered. He felt her slight hesitation and he thought she might pull away. Instead, her hands moved to his waist and her lips opened, offering up her wet heat and sweet tongue.

Desire became a visceral thing—an all-consuming need that blocked out every thought and every memory.

There was no past.

There was just here and now.

There was just Everly.

He drew her closer, his hands tangling in the silky tresses of her hair as he hungrily kissed her. She hungrily kissed him back. Their lips fed as their tongues danced. She moaned deep in her throat and her hands slipped into the back pockets of his jeans, gripping his butt cheeks as if she didn't plan on ever letting him go. He didn't want to let her go either. He wanted this kiss to last for—

"Henry! Henry!"

Paisley's anxious yells had Chance and Everly pulling apart. Everly stared at him with a horrified look for a long second before she turned and ran toward her sister's voice. He quickly followed. When he came around the corner of the row of trees, he saw Paisley running toward them.

"It's Henry," she said. "He ran off and I can't find him."

"It's okay," Chance said. "He couldn't have gone far. He's probably playing hide-and-seek in these trees. That's something Shane and I would've done. Everly, you check the first two rows. Paisley, you check the next two. And I'll check the others. Yell when you find him."

They all spread out. Chance took his time searching between and under every tree on each row. When he finished with his rows and hadn't heard Everly or Paisley yell, he started to grow concerned. There was a long ravine not more than a hundred feet away. Had Henry fallen into it? Chance hadn't prayed for anything for himself in a long time, but he started praying now as he headed out of the trees and ran for the ravine. Before he could get there, a horse and rider came riding out from the corpse of trees next to the ravine. As the cowboy grew closer, Chance saw that it was Hayden West. Sitting in the saddle in front of Hayden was a grinning Henry.

"Look at me, Pastor Chance! I'm a cowboy!"

At Henry's yell, Everly and Paisley both came running out of the trees as Hayden drew the horse to a stop.

"Did anyone lose a cowpoke?" Hayden asked with a smile. His smile faded when Paisley charged toward the horse.

"Henry!"

The horse startled and reared. Chance dove at Paisley and pulled her back from the flailing hooves as Hayden held tight to Henry and worked to control the horse. Once he had control, he chastised Paisley. "What are you doing, woman? You don't ever run at a horse. Not only could you have gotten trampled, but me and this child could've been thrown off."

Paisley was always so soft spoken so Chance was surprised when she snapped back. "I wasn't running at a horse. I was running to my son—my son who has no business being on that beast."

"Calm down, Paise," Everly said. "Hayden would never do anything to harm Henry. I told you about Hayden. He helps me out at the bar."

"I don't care who he is. I want Henry off that horse. Now!"

"Yes, ma'am." Hayden dismounted and then lifted Henry down. Henry didn't look happy, but he seemed to be as surprised by his mother's outburst as everyone else was. He didn't say a word as Paisley took his hand and pulled him toward the Christmas trees.

"Sorry about that, Hayden," Everly said. "My sister was just scared for her son."

Hayden nodded. "I get it. Mama bears don't like anyone messing with their cubs." He watched Paisley until she disappeared into the rows of Christmas trees before he turned back to Everly. "How did she get the bruises?"

"Long story that's not mine to tell. Now I better go check on her." She winked. "Thanks for saving my nephew, hot rodeo cowboy. I owe you."

While her using the word hot with him had left Chance with a warm glow, her using it with

Hayden left him feeling ticked off. He grew even more ticked off when Hayden smiled.

"Are we talking a drink kinda owe or a date kinda owe?"

Everly's gaze met Chance's before it returned to Hayden. "Your choice, cowboy."

# Chapter Fifteen

"I DON'T TRUST HIM."

Everly lowered the dress she'd just pulled out of the closet and turned to see Paisley standing in the doorway of her room. Her bruises on the outside had faded, but after Paisley's uncharacteristic explosion at the Kingman Ranch, Everly knew her sister's inside bruises were still tender and raw.

"I assume you're talking about Hayden."

Paisley moved into the room. "I don't trust him and I think it would be a mistake to go out with him."

Everly had been thinking the same thing since agreeing to the date. She liked Hayden. And unlike her sister, she trusted him. She even thought he was hot . . . just not as hot as a certain preacher. Which was exactly why she'd agreed to go out with him. She needed to make a point to that hot preacher—and to herself—that the kisses they had shared meant nothing. Not a damn thing.

Even if they had.

When she had suggested he needed to kiss a few girls to prove to himself that he was still a virile man, she hadn't meant her. Something happened when she and Chance kissed. Something that hadn't happened with any other man. It wasn't just that he was a great kisser and knew how to make her burn. It was something more than just sexual. When his lips touched her, she felt emotional. Like she either wanted to burst into tears or start spouting love sonnets.

It was terrifying.

Because she knew that whatever was happening between them was not going to end well. They might enjoy each other's company and ignite whenever they touched, but they were two complete opposites. She was the bad girl and he was the good boy. She liked to break the rules and he liked to follow them.

At least, he had followed them until Lori passed away. Then he had gotten a little off track. But Everly knew once he stopped grieving, he'd return to the rule-following preacher she had first met. She didn't fit with perfectionists who followed the rules. Her childhood had proved it.

Which meant she needed to stop whatever was happening between her and Chance and she needed to stop it now. She was hoping the date with Hayden would do it. He was picking her up after rehearsals and taking her for a late dinner in Amarillo. She had asked him to pick her up at the church to make a point to Chance. She was not falling for another Ransom.

She took the red dress off the hanger. "Hayden is a good guy, Paise. You just don't know him."

"And how well can you know him? Chance

told me that he just showed up in town one day."

She turned to Paisley. "You talked about Hayden with Chance?"

Paisley sat down on the bed and scooped up Scuttle to cuddle. The other two kittens were tumbling around on the floor near Everly's feet. "Why does that surprise you? Chance and I talk about other things than my life with Jonathan. He's easy to talk to."

Everly wasn't sure why she suddenly felt a stab of jealousy. She was glad Paisley had become friends with Chance. And who knew? Maybe they would become more than just friends. Paisley was perfect for Chance. They were both rule followers.

She slipped the dress over her head to hide any residual jealousy. "Chance is a good man. You should consider going out with him once your divorce is final."

"After Jonathan, I don't want to go out with any man. But especially a man who is interested in my sister."

Everly popped her head out of the dress. "What?"

"Chance likes you."

"He said that?"

Paisley smiled. "He didn't have to. The man can't keep his eyes off you. And while he's always a good listener when I'm pouring my heart and soul out, he perks up even more when I talk about you."

"Exactly what have you been telling him about me?"

"Just that you were always the light everyone gravitated to."

Everly stared at her. "The light everyone gravitated to? That was you. I was the hellion who anyone with half a brain avoided."

"The only people who avoided you were Mom and Dad. And it was because they were scared that your light and warmth might melt their cold exteriors and expose them for the frauds they are." Paisley looked down at Scuttle asleep in her lap. "I was scared of that too."

"You weren't a fraud, Paise. You were just a kid trying to make your parents happy."

"By pretending to be a perfect princess when I wasn't. But you refused to pretend. You looked our parents in the eyes and said, 'Here I am. Take me or leave me.' I never had the strength to do that. Not with teachers, or our parents, or Jonathan. I don't even know who I am. But you do, Ev. You know who you are and you know what you want."

Everly snorted. "I've yet to figure out what I want. Look at me. I'm living above a bar in a Podunk town."

Paisley smiled. "And you're happy. You've always been a small-town girl."

"What? Are you crazy? I don't even like small towns."

"What you didn't like was living in a house where you couldn't be yourself. But you loved living in Mesaville. Every time we rode our bikes through town, you'd be waving and grinning like you were in a parade. You knew everyone's name and would ask about their kids or their dogs or their garden."

Everly's memories had been so tied up in her failure as a daughter she hadn't given much thought to the time she spent away from her parents. Now those memories came flooding back: Learning to crochet with the next-door neighbor, Mrs. Goodwin. Helping Mr. Peterson weed his garden. Getting ice cream sundaes from Wally Matheson who worked at the soda fountain.

"Remember Wally Matheson?" she asked. "He had such a crush on you that he gave me free sundaes."

Paisley laughed. "He gave you free sundaes because he had a crush on you. Not me."

"Me?" Everly stared at her sister. "But you were closer to his age and the perfect angel."

Paisley's smile faded. "Yes, and perfect angels are nice to look at, but they're not much fun to hang out with. Which is why I didn't have many friends or boyfriends growing up. But you did, Everly. Everyone wanted to be with you." She hesitated. "Even my own son would rather be with you than me."

Everly sat down on the bed and took her sister's hands. "That's not true, Paise. Henry adores you."

"Only because I give him anything he wants. I'm so afraid of being like our parents that I went the opposite way and spoil him rotten."

Everly couldn't argue the point. "You've had a

lot to deal with. Once you've had some time to get your life sorted out, you can set down rules for Henry. For now, you just need to heal."

Tears filled Paisley's eyes. "Will I?"

"Of course you will. It just takes time. Now how about if you come with me to rehearsals? Your bruises are faded. With some makeup, no one will know the difference."

Paisley shook her head. "I still need a little time before I meet the townsfolk."

"Okay, but you're coming with me on Thursday night. It will be the dress rehearsal and you'll want to see Henry in his Tiny Sidewinder Tim costume."

Paisley laughed. "That I can't miss." She set Scuttle on the bed and got up. "Now, I better go rescue Hester. She's baking sugar cut-out cookies with Henry and I'm sure he's already talked her ear off."

As soon as Paisley left, Everly finished getting dressed. After fixing her hair and applying makeup, she put the kittens in their room and headed downstairs. She had a slice of the new holiday pies Gretchen had dropped by yesterday—Chocolate Candy Cane Surprise—before driving across the street to pick up Henry at the Malones'. He was even more talkative than usual, probably due to the sugar cookies he'd eaten. She listened with half an ear as she mentally prepared herself for seeing Chance.

*Just paste on a smile and act like the kiss at the Kingmans' Ranch meant nothing.*

Unfortunately, her mind forgot all about the

pep talk when she stepped into the church and saw Chance standing next to the Christmas tree in the foyer. Her stomach felt like it dropped ten floors while her heart felt like it floated straight up to the ceiling.

When his dark coffee eyes landed on her, they held a look that burned right through her and incinerated the calm, collected woman who was going to act like the kiss had meant nothing. She tripped over the threshold.

Chance hurried over to steady her. "Easy there." The touch of his hand on her arm made her feel even more unsteady. She couldn't stop her gaze from lowering to his mouth.

"Is that star for our tree, Pastor Chance?" Henry's question had Chance releasing Everly and looking down at her nephew. Which gave her time to collect herself. Or try to.

"As a matter of fact, it is," Chance said. "When Mr. Olson, Mrs. Moody, and I were decorating the tree, I realized we didn't have a star. And what's a Christmas tree without a star? So I ordered one online and it just came in today. Would you like to help me put it on?"

"Sure! But how am I gonna get up there?"

"I have an idea." Chance handed Henry the star and then lifted him up to his shoulders. The smile on Henry's face said it all. Chance was smiling too.

Everly's heart felt like it was being squeezed in a giant fist and her eyes filled with tears. She blinked them away, but they came right back when Henry leaned over to put the star on the top of the tree. After he finished, Chance set him down and they both looked at the tree.

"Do you know why we put stars on Christmas trees, Henry?" Chance asked.

"'Cause they're pretty?"

"Yes, but also because a brilliant star was what hung over the manger where Jesus was born. It's what guided the shepherds and wise men to Him."

"I love stars. And I love Christmas trees."

Chance hesitated before he spoke. "Me too." He glanced over at Everly. "What do you think, Everly?"

As she looked at Chance standing next to the tree with his dark brown eyes reflecting the twinkle lights and his hand resting on Henry's shoulder, she thought she was in big trouble.

Thankfully, before she had to answer, the door opened and Kitty, Hester, and Mystic swept in. Of course, Kitty was talking. She talked as much as Henry. Everly realized she'd grown just as attached to the woman's jabbering.

"All I can say is that Potts stinks at courtin'. His idea of a date is me watching him cook. I love to eat, but occasionally I'd like my man to pay more attention to me than he does to his sautéed onions. And since Mystic hasn't seen any love aura around him when we're together, I figured he's just not that interested."

"Just because I didn't see an aura doesn't mean he doesn't like you, Kitty," Mystic said as she took off her jacket. "I don't see auras until feelings start getting serious. And you two haven't been dating long."

Kitty snorted. "We haven't been dating at all. Is it too much to ask for a nice candlelight dinner and a man who isn't working in the kitchen preparing the food?" She glanced over and finally noticed Everly, Chance, and Henry. "Well, hey, y'all. I didn't see you standing there. And would you look at that tree? That's about the prettiest tree I ever did see."

"I chopped it down!" Henry yelled. "And put on the star!"

Hester smiled. "Then no wonder it looks so beautiful. Your help certainly made the sugar cookies twice as pretty. In fact, they turned out so good, I brought some for you to share with all the other children." She pulled a Tupperware container out of the tote bag she carried. Henry immediately raced over.

"Can I pass them out, Hessy?"

"You sure can. Just be careful or you'll have nothing but crumbs."

Henry carefully took the container. "I'm gonna take them up to the Sunday school room right now."

Everly started to follow him up the stairs, but Chance placed a hand on her arm. "Mrs. Moody is up there. She'll keep an eye on him."

She didn't care if Mrs. Moody was in the Sunday school room. She wasn't worried about Henry getting into trouble as much as she needed a few minutes to collect her thoughts. But with Chance's hand on her arm, it was hard to put two words together. She didn't know how long she would have stood there like a speechless idiot if Mystic hadn't released a startled gasp.

Chance let go of Everly's arm and they both turned to find Mystic staring at them with wide eyes.

"Are you okay, Mystic?" Chance asked. "Is it the baby?"

Mystic blinked. "Uhh . . . no. It was just . . . the tree. It's breathtaking."

Everly knew a lie when she heard it. Mystic hadn't even been looking at the tree. She'd been looking at Chance and Everly. Which could only mean one thing.

She'd seen a love aura.

"Holy shit."

The words just slipped out and everyone turned to her.

She cleared her throat. "Sorry . . . but I just realized Henry's probably sitting upstairs eating all the cookies. I better go check." She hurried for the stairs. Once on the second floor, she leaned back against the wall in the hallway and tried to mentally talk herself out of a major panic attack.

She was not in love with Chance. She was NOT. She didn't care if he had turned from a holier-than-thou Scrooge into a really nice guy with sexy scruff and steamy coffee eyes. He was NOT for her.

A thought struck her.

What if the love aura Mystic saw wasn't Everly's? What if it was Chance's? Somehow that seemed even worse. Everly was strong enough to get over another heartbreak, but Chance wasn't. He had just gotten over Lori. He couldn't deal with getting his hopes crushed again. And Everly *would* crush his hopes. Because if he didn't know they didn't belong together, she did.

"Everly?"

She turned to see Chance walking toward her. She took a deep breath and pinned on a smile. "Hey, Preach! I was just . . . catching my breath after climbing the stairs. I guess I need to do more cardio."

He studied her. "What's going on? You've been acting weird since you stepped into the church. This is about the kiss at the Kingman Ranch, isn't it?"

She rolled her eyes. "As if. Do you know how many guys I've kissed? Hundreds."

He tipped his head and sent her a pointed look. "Hundreds?"

"Well, maybe not hundreds. But a lot. So I'm not freaking out about the kiss. I'm freaking out that you got the wrong idea about the kiss. When I said that you needed to get back in the game and kiss some girls, I meant other girls. Not me. You don't want to get back into the game with me because we don't play by the same rules and someone's bound to get hurt."

Like a preacher who just got over losing his wife.

She only thought the words, but somehow he read her mind.

"Like me."

"Yes, like you. And like me. I just got over

Shane—your brother, in case you forgot. And both of us need time to heal before we jump back into a relationship. So let's just forget the kiss, or kisses, ever happened and move on."

His gaze lowered to her mouth. "I don't think I can do that."

She swallowed hard and tried to ignore the pool of heat that settled in her stomach. "Of course you can. You just need to get back in the saddle and start dating. Not just one girl, but lots of girls. You need to get some experience under your belt, Preach, before you dive back into a serious relationship."

His gaze lifted. His eyes were hot and needy. He placed a hand on the wall next to her head and stepped close. "You're right. I do need experience." He lowered his head and kissed her.

# Chapter Sixteen

CHANCE UNDERSTOOD WHAT was happening. Everly was scared she was going to hurt him. He had to admit he was scared too. But he couldn't stop whatever was happening between them. And he no longer wanted to.

For a brief second, her mouth stayed closed. Then her lips parted and she welcomed him into heaven. She tasted like a chocolate-covered candy cane—a mixture of comforting sweetness and naughty decadence. Which described Everly to a tee. She was comforting sweetness all wrapped up in naughty decadence. He craved her. He craved her like he had never craved another woman. If they had been anywhere else, he would have continued to kiss her. But they weren't. Any second, they could be discovered.

Regretfully, he drew away.

Her eyes fluttered open. It was like looking into two blazing fires. They made him feel scorched . . . and completely warm and happy.

Unfortunately, she didn't seem to feel the same way.

She looked confused and angry. "No." She

shook her head. "Absolutely not. Do you understand me? Just no!" She pushed past him and headed down the hall toward the stairs.

He started to go after her, but then Mrs. Moody and Henry came out of the Sunday school room. Since it was time for the rehearsal to start, Chance would have to wait to talk to Everly.

But they would talk.

He could no longer deny his attraction to her. And it was obvious she was attracted to him too. Now the question was what should they do about it? Everly was right. They were complete opposites who played by different rules. Chance had too many rules and Everly seemed to have none. The smart thing to do would be to accept that and back off. But what had being smart and playing by the rules ever gotten him? It certainly hadn't gotten him love and happiness. For once, he didn't want to play by the rules. For once, he wanted to just let life happen.

The rehearsal went surprisingly well. Besides Henry and a few of the younger children, everyone knew their lines and songs and needed very little directing.

Which was a good thing since Chance was totally preoccupied with Everly.

She looked sexy as hell in the red dress and he couldn't seem to take his eyes off her. The low neckline showed off her heart tattoo and the short hem showed off her long legs. A silver zipper ran down the back and made him think about things he had no business thinking about. Especially in church. It was a relief when the rehearsal was over and people started getting on their coats.

Chance walked over to the piano where Everly was talking with Mrs. Moody. "I was wondering if you could stay a few minutes after, Everly."

She got up from the piano bench and busily collected the music sheets. "Sorry, Preach, but I have a date."

Chance was stunned speechless. When she'd agreed to a date with Hayden the other day at the Kingman Ranch, he'd thought she had just been doing what she always did with men. Flirting. Obviously that wasn't the case. Before he could react, Mrs. Moody spoke.

"A date? With whom?"

"Hayden West."

So that explained the red dress and heels when she normally wore leggings and a tank top to rehearsal. For some reason, Chance had thought she'd worn the dress for him. He felt stupid ... and extremely jealous. He stood there not knowing what to say or do.

"If you'll excuse me," Mrs. Moody said. "There's something I need to discuss with Hester and Kitty." She hurried over to where the two women were talking and the three ladies put their heads together and started whispering while Chance returned his attention to Everly.

"A date?"

"Yeah, you know that thing two people go on when they like each other."

"And you like Hayden?"

She looked away and picked up her coat that

was lying on the piano. "What woman wouldn't like a hot rodeo cowboy?"

He studied her. "I know what you're doing."

"What's that?"

"You think that dating someone else will stop whatever is happening between us."

She turned back to him. "There's nothing happening between us, Preach."

He took the coat from her and held it out. She hesitated for a second before slipping her arms into it. As he slid the coat over her shoulders, he felt her slight tremble. He leaned in and whispered next to her ear. "There's something happening between us, Everly. Something I don't think a date with another man is going to fix."

Before Everly could reply, Hester walked up. "Diana Moody said that you have a date with Hayden, Everly."

Everly turned and shot Chance an annoyed look before she answered Hester. "As a matter of fact, I do. He's taking me to dinner in Amarillo."

"Hmm? I don't think traveling that far is a good idea." She touched the crystal hanging around her neck. "I've been seeing snow lately."

Everly laughed. "In Texas? I wouldn't bet on that prediction. When was the last time you got snow here in—"

Before she could finish, Hester clasped the stone and went completely still. "Paisley's in trouble."

Everly's laughter faded. "What do you mean? What kind of trouble?"

Hester rubbed the crystal between her fingers as she stared vacantly at Everly. "I don't know.

I just see her surrounded by an ominous dark cloud. I think you and Chance need to get over to the house now. Kitty, Diana, and I will stay with Henry."

Everly didn't hesitate to head for the door. Chance quickly followed behind her. When they got outside, he placed a hand on her arm.

"Calm down, Everly. We don't know for sure Paisley's in trouble. After all, Hester predicted snow and we both know that's unlikely to happen."

"I'm still going to check on her." She pulled open the door of her car and got in while Chance jumped into the passenger's seat. He barely got his seat belt on before she backed out in a squeal of tires and took off out of the parking lot.

"Slow down," Chance said as he held on to the dashboard.

"Don't tell me what to do, Preach." She shot him an annoyed look. "Just because we kissed doesn't mean you're in charge of me. I don't need your permission to drive fast. Or to date."

"I don't want to be in charge of you. I just want you to—"

She cut him off. "Change? Because that's not happening, Preach. I am who I am. A tattooed, cussing, drinking, fast-driving woman who isn't going to change for anyone!"

"I don't want you to change."

She glanced at him. "Really? Then what do you want?"

He didn't even have to think about it. "You. I want you. Exactly the way you are. You're right. It doesn't make sense. You're the complete opposite of everything I thought I wanted in a woman."

"You mean the complete opposite of Lori."

He couldn't deny it. "What's wrong with that? What's wrong with me wanting someone completely different from Lori?"

"Because a woman like Lori *is* exactly what you want. Grieving has screwed up your head and made you think you want something you don't."

"You're right. Ever since Lori died, my head has been screwed up. I didn't have a clue who I was or what I believed or where my life was going. I'm still confused about those things. But what I'm not confused about is you, Everly. You're the only thing I know for sure that I want. The one clear thought in my head. The one light strong enough to shine through all the darkness."

He waited for her say something. Anything. Or at least turn to him. Instead, she stared straight ahead, her hands tight on the steering wheel. When she finally spoke, it had nothing to do with his soul-revealing speech.

"Whose SUV is that?"

Chance followed her gaze to the car parked in front of the Malones. "I don't know. I've never seen it before."

"Me neither." She sped up and pulled into the dirt lot next to the Malones' house so fast that her back tires skidded. She parked by the porch and they both jumped out. She got up the steps first, but he pushed past her before she could reach the door.

"Let me go first." He opened the door without knocking and walked in.

Hester had been right. Paisley was in trouble. A man had her shoved against the wall with his hand around her throat. His next words identified him as Paisley's husband, Jonathan.

"You can't leave me, you stupid bitch! I won't let you."

Chance started toward them. But before he could get there, Everly exploded past him and attacked Jonathan.

"Let go of my sister, you asshole!"

Jonathan released Paisley and turned on Everly, who was throwing punches like a prizefighter in the last round. Worried she was going to hurt herself, Chance placed an arm around her waist and tried to hold her back. But of course, she continued swinging.

"I'm going to kill you, you bastard."

"Stop punching me, you bitch!" Jonathan drew back his fist and Chance barely had time to pull Everly out of the way before he swung. The punch clipped Chance on the corner of his eye and had him stumbling back. He caught his balance and retaliated with a right to Jonathan's jaw that knocked him back. He recovered quickly and charged Chance. Before Chance could deliver another blow, Hayden came through the open door and rammed Jonathan back against the wall. He pinned him there with a forearm to his throat.

"What the hell is going on?" Hayden's gaze zeroed in on Paisley who was standing there looking stunned with Jonathan's fingerprints on her neck. Hayden looked back at Jonathan and must have pressed harder on his throat because the man's eyes bulged. "Since I'm sure you have rules about doing unto others, preacher, why don't you let me take care of the trash."

Before Chance could reply, Paisley spoke. "It's my problem. I'll take care of it." She turned to Everly. "Call the police, Ev. I'm pressing charges."

It was close to midnight by the time the sheriff left with Jonathan in tow. Chance doubted the sheriff could keep him in jail for longer than one night. But at least Paisley had filed charges so there was a record of Jonathan's abuse. It would help in the custody case. Although Jonathan hadn't mentioned Henry once when talking to the sheriff. He was obviously drunk and just kept repeating that Paisley was his wife—like she was some kind of property he owned and it was okay he had abused her. Chance figured this wasn't the last time they'd see Jonathan in Cursed.

Hayden seemed to agree.

While they were standing in the yard watching the tow truck Everly had called haul off Jonathan's SUV, Hayden spoke. "That man won't be gotten rid of this easily. We'll have to keep a close eye on Paisley and Henry."

Chance glanced over at him. "We?"

Hayden nodded. "I figure Paisley can use all the guardian angels she can get right now."

Once the tow truck and Hayden left, Chance went inside to find Everly arguing with her sister.

"Stop being such a pain in the ass, Paise. You're

coming back to the bar with me and that's final. We'll make cocoa and eat some chocolate peppermint pie and watch those sappy Hallmark Christmas romances you love."

Paisley smiled. "I don't love those movies. You do."

"Okay, then we'll watch something else. I just don't want you being alone tonight." Hester had called earlier and she and Paisley had agreed that it would be best if Hester took Henry to the Kingman Ranch for the night so he wouldn't see his father carted off in handcuffs. Chance agreed Paisley shouldn't be left alone, but she appeared to be as stubborn as her sister when she'd made up her mind.

"I'm not going to spend the night at the bar, Everly."

"Then I'll stay here."

Paisley shook her head. "I need some time alone to process everything. I promise I'll call you first thing in the morning."

Everly looked like she was about to argue, but then conceded. "You're not just going to call me, you're going to get donuts with me and Henry in the morning." She gave Paisley a tight hug. "I love you, Paise."

"I love you too, Ev. Thanks for coming to my rescue." Paisley smiled at Chance over Everly's shoulder. "You too, Chance."

"You have Hester to thank for that." Chance would never doubt the woman's psychic powers again.

After Chance made sure all the doors and

windows were locked, he followed Everly out to the car. It was easy to read the concern on her face as she started the engine.

"She's going to be okay, Everly," he said. "Jonathan won't be released until the morning and he'll still have to get his SUV from the tow company."

"I'm not worried about him coming back tonight. I'm just worried about my sister. I feel so helpless."

"You're doing everything you can do. All you can do now is be there for her and Henry." He thought about what Hester had told him. "A wise woman once told me that when you're grieving, the best cure is to be surrounded by people who love and care about you."

"But Paisley's not grieving."

"Yes, she is. She's grieving all the hopes and dreams she had for the future."

Everly glanced over at him as she put the car into drive. "Is that what you grieve, Preach? Your hopes and dreams for the future?"

He nodded. "Every married couple has hopes and dreams. Kids, traveling, growing old together. And when those hopes are gone, it leaves you floundering and terrified of ever hoping again. You have to start small. One hope at a time."

She stared at him for a long moment before she released the brake and headed for the main street. He expected her to take him to the church where his truck was parked. Instead, she pulled into Nasty Jack's parking lot.

"What are you doing?" he asked.

"Your eye is starting to swell. You need to get ice on it."

He didn't mention that he had ice back at his house.

Once inside the bar, Everly led him up the stairs to her room. She sat him on the bed and then disappeared. When she returned, she carried a huge bag of frozen French fries. Three little kittens followed behind her.

"Lie back on the pillows," she ordered.

He did as instructed and she placed the bag over his entire face. "This is freezing," he mumbled into the icy bag.

"Leave it there." Three soft balls of fur were set on his chest before he felt his foot being lifted and his boot tugged off.

"What are you doing?"

"Making you more comfortable." She tugged his other boot off. Then he heard the pad of her feet leaving the room, followed by the sound of running water. He was about to remove the frozen fries when she returned.

"You take orders well. I like that in a man."

He smiled and stroked the kittens that were curled on his chest in a furry tangle. "I feel like you're planning something devious."

"I am."

The mattress sank at the foot of the bed, and a second later, Everly's body snuggled next to his side. Her head rested on his shoulder and her bare leg hooked over his. She joined him petting the cats, her fingers brushing his every so often. Even with a cold bag of fries over his eyes, he felt content. More content than he'd felt in a long time.

After a while, Everly spoke. "Thanks for being there tonight, Preach."

"You're welcome. Sorry your date with Hayden was ruined."

"No, you're not."

"You're right. I'm not."

She laughed, but quickly sobered. "We would make the oddest couple ever. You know that, right?"

"I do."

She stopped petting the kittens and slipped an arm around his waist, snuggling closer. "As long as you know it."

She fell asleep immediately, her breath falling against the side of his neck in soft, even puffs. He should get up and leave. But he didn't. He just lay there with the bag of fries over his face and the kittens purring on his chest and the soft woman cuddling his side until he too fell asleep.

When he woke, the frozen fries were gone and the purplish light of dawn spilled in through the window. As he came more fully awake, he began to notice other things. The subtle, seductive smell that always surrounded Everly now surrounded him, and something slid over his chest. Not kitten fur, but something longer and silkier. Amid the slide of silk were soft, light brushes—along his collarbone, in the hollow of his throat, down the middle of his breastbone.

He glanced down and saw a pile of fiery waves. One word came out of his mouth in a hushed whisper.

"Everly."

# Chapter Seventeen

EVERLY SHOULD STOP now. She could play off unsnapping his shirt and taking a taste of his warm skin as just a moment of sleep-deprived insanity. Except she didn't feel sleep deprived. And she didn't feel insane. And she certainly didn't want to stop. Being here with Chance felt right. More right than anything had ever felt in her life. That feeling of rightness only grew stronger when he slipped his fingers through her hair and drew her up to his waiting lips.

The kiss the night before had been greedy and rushed. This morning, his kiss was slow and leisurely. As if he had all the time in the world to savor her. His lips sipped while his tongue lazily dipped into her mouth in a slow exploration that left her breathless and lightheaded. She was lying fully on top of him. Her soft breasts rested on his hard pectoral muscles. Her stomach rested on his warm naked abs. And the part of her that felt all achy rested on the rough denim of his fly.

She could feel the thump of his heart, the flex of his abs . . . and the growing ridge of his desire. Lust was too mild a word for the feeling that flooded her. She'd felt ordinary lust before, but the heated waves that crashed through her body weren't ordinary. She had to face the fact that she wanted this man like she had never wanted another man. When he slipped a hand over her butt cheek and pressed her against his denim-covered erection, she whimpered with need.

"I got you, baby," he whispered against her lips as he held her in place and rocked his hips. She literally saw stars. Or at least little dots of light as her eyes rolled back in her head.

Needing more pressure, she opened her legs and adjusting her hips until his hard length was right where she wanted it. Then she met the next rock of his hips with a roll of her own. The friction had them both moaning. They continued the bump and grind until Chance pulled away from the kiss, his eyes hot and his breath ragged.

"Everly, stop, baby."

She kept right on pumping, hoping to alleviate the building ache. But before she could, he rolled her over to her back. She started to complain, but stopped when his hand slipped into her panties. The feel of his warm fingers had her sighing as his fingers delved and explored until they found the spot that needed touching the most. They soothed the ache with a quick up-and-down stroke that sent her flying. Then he drew out the orgasm with slow, gentle brushes of his fingertips. As the last tingles faded, she opened her eyes and smiled.

"Not bad for an inexperienced preacher."

He answered her smile with a dazzling one of

his own before he kissed her and then got out of bed.

She leaned up on her elbows and stared at him. "What are you doing? Because if you think I'm finished with you, Preach, you've got another think coming."

He laughed. "I have no intentions of going anywhere." He slipped off his unsnapped shirt, revealing all his glorious muscles, then reached for the button of his jeans.

She got to her feet and stopped him. "In that case, I'll be happy to help."

But instead of unbuttoning his jeans, she enjoyed the bare skin that was already exposed. Starting at his clavicle, she traced the distinct bone to the hollow of his throat and back again. Then spreading her fingers wide, she slid her hands along his shoulders and down to his biceps.

"You have an amazing body, Preach. Did you know that?"

His words came out breathy and sexy as hell. "I bet you say that to all the boys."

She laughed as she explored his hard chest. "Only the ones who do."

She covered his hard pecs with her hands. The muscles flexed beneath her palms and she gave them a squeeze before brushing her thumbs over his nipples. His head tipped back, his features etched with desire. She slipped one hand down his washboard stomach and flipped open the button of his jeans. Then inch by inch, she slid down his zipper, releasing his straining, cotton-covered erection.

It was impressive.

She used one fingernail to trace the thick outline through the cotton. "Did I do this to you?"

He sharply sucked in his breath. "Everly. I'm on the edge here."

She sat down on the bed and, hooking two fingers in the elastic band of his briefs, pulled him between her spread legs. She smiled up at him wickedly. "Now we can't have that." She lowered his briefs until he sprung free. Her breath hitched. Oh, yes, he was impressive. She caressed the rigid length from pulsing base to moist tip.

"Ev-verly."

"Shh, Preach. I'm busy." She traced around the tip and back down to the base before taking him in hand. As she stroked, the sound Chance made was half moan and half sigh. She wondered how long it had been since a woman had touched him. Loved him. Not that this was love. But it was something more than sex. She had never felt this way before. Never felt like she wanted to please a man more than she pleased herself.

Maybe it was selfishness, but she wanted him to remember tonight. She didn't doubt for a second that he would remarry. But in life's ordinary, dull moments, she wanted him to remember this. She wanted him to remember her. She lowered her head and took him into her mouth.

His fingers slid into her hair and he guided her for a few strokes before he fisted his hands and pulled her away.

"Not yet, Ev," he said. He stepped out of his

jeans and briefs before tugging off his socks. Completely naked, his body was more than impressive. It was breathtaking.

"Damn, Preach. If the women of this town knew what you were hiding beneath those conservative suits and starched shirts, they'd be beating down your door."

He caressed his fingers along her jaw and tipped her head so she was looking up at him. "Like I told you before, I'm not interested in other women. I'm interested in you." He leaned down and kissed her. She melted into his kiss, her hands slipping over the firm cheeks of his butt.

After several drugging kisses, he drew back and slipped her tank top over her head. His gaze lowered to her breasts. He stared at them for what felt like forever before he reverently lifted a hand and gently cradled one in his palm. It was sexy, but also comforting . . . until his thumb strummed over her nipple, igniting a shower of sparks through her body.

The sparks became flaming torches when he knelt in front of her and took one aching nub into his hot, wet mouth. She expected a suckle. Possibly a brush of tongue. She did not expect him to run the edge of his bottom teeth across it and take a nip. The slight pain was quickly washed away with the brush of his tongue.

Her head drooped and she fisted his hair, holding him to her breast as he continued to torture her with teeth and tongue and mouth. When she was nothing but a puddle of quivering need, he lifted her back to the mattress and kissed his way down her stomach. He stopped at her belly button ring, brushing his tongue over each stud.

"Do you know how insane these two little diamonds have made me?" He took the top stud between his teeth and tugged. She moaned from the heat it ignited. While he tongue-played with her belly button ring, his fingers slipped in the elastic of her panties and tugged them down. Then his lips moved lower and did something she didn't think preachers did.

But Chance did it.

And he did it well.

His skilled lips and tongue had her trembling and quickly tumbling into another amazing orgasm. While her body was still quivering from release, he entered her with a hard thrust that either prolonged her orgasm or gave her another one. She wasn't quite sure which. All she knew was that she didn't want him to stop.

As he continued to thrust and send heat waves ricocheting through her, she started rambling incoherent words. "So good . . . it's so good. Yes, Chance! Harder . . . yes. Oh, yes!" By the time Chance climaxed and she'd drifted down from the best sexual orgasm of her life, she was feeling more than a little embarrassed.

She had never rambled during sex. Never.

But it turned out she did a lot of things with Chance she'd never done before. She'd never been a cuddler after sex. But when he shifted off her and pulled her into his arms, she was too content to move. She'd never slept with a guy before, but as his hand brushed up and down her arm in a soft caress, her eyelids fluttered closed and she drifted off to sleep.

She woke to a nuzzle of wet nose. She opened her eyes to see Flounder's tiny tiger-striped face. Since the kitten always woke her, she pulled the cat close before she snuggled into the pillow. A pillow that smelled like . . .

"Shit!" She sat straight up in bed as Chance walked into the room wearing nothing but his briefs and a smile.

He stopped short at her exclamation and lifted his eyebrows. "Something wrong?"

Everything was wrong. She had made a pledge to stay away from him and she had broken that pledge. And she had no one to blame but herself. She should have never brought him back here. But he had taken a punch for her and she hadn't been able to just drop him off at his house when his eye was swelling.

Of course, she didn't have to reward him with sex either. But it was too late to go back. The damage had already been done. All she could do now was act like it had been no big deal.

"No. Nothing's wrong." She looked at the cups he held. "Is that coffee?"

"It is." He sat down on the edge of the bed and held out a cup. "Although I don't know if I made it to your specifications. I only know how to make pod coffee."

"That's not coffee."

"So I've heard." He stacked some pillows next

to her and got back in bed. Once he was leaning against the pillows, the kittens all clambered onto his lap. He laughed and gave them ear scratches as he took a sip of coffee and sighed. "You're right. It is better."

Okay, this was weird. Why was he lying in her bed and acting like he had no intentions of leaving? And why was he so calm and collected? He'd had sex with a woman he wasn't married to. Wasn't there some kind of preacher rule about that? Shouldn't he be freaked out about breaking that rule?

She sat up and set her coffee on the nightstand before she turned to him. His gaze immediately lowered to her naked breasts. Her nipples hardened. Which freaked her out even more. All it had taken was one glance, and she wanted him all over again. This was not good, and it needed to stop.

She tugged the sheet up and held it to her breasts. "I think we need to talk about what happened this morning."

His gaze lifted and he smiled. "It was amazing."

She blushed. She actually blushed. What was wrong with her?

She cleared her throat. "Well, yes, but it shouldn't have happened. And I take full responsibility. You were sleeping quite contentedly until I crawled on top of you like some . . . wanton hussy."

He set down his coffee on the nightstand and turned to her. "I know how much you enjoy playing Evil Everly, but I wanted to have sex as much as you did. Maybe even more so. If I'm honest, I've lusted after you for a long time. Since college, in fact."

She blinked. "You lusted after me in college?"

He nodded casually as if he hadn't just dropped a huge emotional bomb. "Which probably explained why I judged you so harshly. You were a temptation I knew I couldn't resist if you showed me any interest."

"But college was before Lori?"

He nodded. "Which is another reason I treated you so badly when you got to Cursed. I felt guilty about lusting after you."

She was completely broadsided and it took her a moment to get back on track. A long moment.

"Everly? Are you okay?"

"Yeah . . . I just. Umm . . . where was I?"

One corner of his mouth tipped in a cute half smile. "You were taking full blame for this morning and I was saying that I wanted you as much as you wanted me."

"Oh . . . well, now that we both know it was just lust, we can—"

He cut her off. "I don't think it was just lust."

Talk about freaked out.

She stared at him with wide eyes. "Don't you do it, Preach. Don't you dare make more out of what happened because you can't live with yourself for having casual sex. And that's what it was. Casual sex from bottled-up lust. We both hadn't had sex in a long time and we needed to blow off some steam. And now that it's released, we can go our separate ways. I can go back to Dallas and you can stay here and find someone who is much better suited for you."

He studied her. "I think this morning proved that we suit each other quite well."

She completely lost it. "No, it didn't! It proved nothing except we're good in bed. But out of bed, we're as compatible as a choirboy and a hooker."

"You're not a hooker and I'm certainly not a choirboy. If you're worried about dating a preacher, don't be. I'm quitting after the first of the year."

She stared at him. "You're quitting Holy Gospel?"

"I'm quitting pastoring altogether."

She knew he had been thinking about quitting before, but that was when he had been angry with God. He wasn't angry anymore. It was obvious in the inspirational sermon he'd given on Sunday, and the Christmas tree in the church foyer, and his daily counseling sessions with Paisley, and his enjoyment of directing the play. The last couple weeks, he'd been happy. She knew it didn't just have to do with her. It had to do with regaining his faith.

What did have to do with her was his quitting. He told her that he didn't want her to change. She believed him. But as much as he didn't want her to change, he also believed that who she was wouldn't work for a preacher's wife. He was right. She would never be as perfect as Lori.

She got out of bed and grabbed the robe hanging off the edge of the closet door and tugged it on. "You are *not* quitting, Chance Ransom. And you sure as hell aren't quitting because you want to close the huge chasm between who you are and who I am. You can't change me into someone who fits better in your life. And you certainly shouldn't change yourself to fit better in mine. You belong here in Cursed as the pastor of Holy Gospel. You might not think so now, but you'll figure it out sooner or later. One day, you'll meet a woman who will be perfect for you and you'll get married and have a parsonage filled with little angels who you'll lift up to put stars on your Christmas trees. And don't you dare tell me you don't want that because I see it in your eyes every time you look at Henry. And don't tell me you don't want to be a preacher because I see the same look every time you step up to the pulpit. And you can have it all. The perfect job, the perfect wife, the perfect family. All you have to do is pull your head out of your ass and quit chasing after a woman who is all wrong for you." She pointed a finger at the door. "Now get out of my room."

"What?"

"You heard me. Get out. What happened this morning might have meant something to you, Preach, but it meant absolutely nothing to me. It was sex. Amazing sex, but just sex. Plain and simple."

He moved the kittens off his lap and got out of bed. "You don't mean that, Everly. Your tough act might work with other people, but it won't work with me. And I get it. You're scared. I was scared too. Scared of feeling the pain that comes with caring about someone. But I'm not scared anymore. I love—"

She slapped him hard across the face. She didn't know who was more stunned—she or Chance. They both stood there staring at each other for a long moment before he nodded.

"Okay. You need some time." He collected his clothes from the floor before he turned back to her. His brown eyes held a deep sadness. She hated that she had put it there, but it was for his own good. And for hers. He might think he loved her, but he didn't. It was just his strong morals kicking in after they'd had sex. Sex could do that. It could screw with your head and change the way you looked at a person. It had screwed with Everly's head after having sex with Shane. She refused to let it happen again.

So she didn't say a word when he gave her that sad puppy dog look. She just stared back at him until he turned and walked out the door. She waited until she heard the outside door close before she finally released the breath she'd been holding and dropped down to the bed.

All three kittens crawled onto her lap and she scooped them up and cuddled them close.

She didn't realize she was crying until Flounder licked a tear from her cheek.

# Chapter Eighteen

"Everly's quitting the play?" Kitty stared at Hester, who had delivered the news.

Since it was the dress rehearsal, both women wore costumes. As the Ghost of Christmas Present, Kitty wore a long green velour bathrobe with a gold rope belt and a holly crown. As the Ghost of Christmas Future, Hester wore what she usually wore—a long black dress—but she had added a veil that hung over her silver hair and partially obscured her violet eyes. The effect was spooky.

"But she can't quit," Kitty continued. "The play is only two days away. And we can't perform *Cowboy Scrooge* without Scrooge!" She looked at Chance. "You have to do something, Reverend."

There was nothing Chance could do. After their night together, Everly had been avoiding him. He'd tried calling her, but she refused to answer or return his calls. He'd tried stopping by to see her, but she wouldn't answer the door during the day and completely ignored him when he went to Nasty Jack's at night. He'd even tried butting in on her and Henry's donut morning at Good Eats. But they never showed up.

He loved her. He knew that now. He didn't know exactly when it had happened: The night she had nursed him back to health. The morning they shared the donut at the diner. The kiss at the Kingman Ranch. Maybe it had been all those moments and all the moments in between. The ones where she had shown him the caring woman beneath her blunt talk and sassy swagger.

He believed she loved him too. But that didn't mean there would be a happily ever after. Once Everly set her mind to something, it was hard to change it. She was convinced they were too opposite to make a relationship work. And maybe she was right. Maybe things would have imploded if they had gotten together. His heart certainly felt like it was imploding now.

"I'll be Cowboy Scooge!" Henry yelled at the top of his lungs. "I'll be Cowboy Scooge!" He tried to jump up and down, but his silvery snake costume fit too snugly around his legs. So all he could do was bounce on his cowboy boots and cause his hat to tip over his eyes.

Hester pushed it back. "But if you're Cowboy Scrooge, someone else will have to be Tiny Sidewinder Tim ... and wear your snake costume."

Henry's eyes widened in horror and he clutched his long tail to his chest. "I'm not gibing up my snake costume."

"Of course you're not," Mrs. Moody said. As the Ghost of Christmas Past, she wore an old-fashioned dress with a wide-brimmed prairie bonnet that dipped when she turned to Hester. "Is there any way we can talk Everly out of quitting?"

Hester shook her head sadly. "I tried, but she stubbornly refused to listen." She glanced at Chance. "She says she's leaving after the holidays."

The ache in his heart grew almost unbearable at just the thought of Everly leaving Cursed. Even if she wouldn't talk to him, at least, when she was here, he could see her. The twinkle in her golden eyes when she teased Shane. The soft smile on her full lips when she cuddled the kittens. The love that came over her beautiful face when she gazed at Paisley and Henry.

"Then I guess you'll just have to be Cowboy Scrooge, Reverend."

Chance blinked out of his thoughts and looked at Mrs. Moody. "Oh, no, I—"

"She's right," Hester said. "You're the only logical choice. You're the only one who knows all the lines and words to the songs."

"Speaking of songs," Kitty said. "I hate to be a party pooper, but the reverend sings about as well as Potts does."

Potts, who was dressed like a destitute Billy Bob Cratchit, stared at Kitty. "What are you talking about, woman? I got a voice like Hank Williams. Senior not Junior."

Kitty snorted. "Have you lost your mind, cowboy? You're about as good at singin' as you are at courtin'. No woman wants to spend all her time in a hot kitchen watching her man slave over a stove."

"That's my job!"

"And my job is delivering mail. But I don't expect you to follow me around delivering packages on our nights together. The Kingmans give you days off for a reason—to get out and enjoy life. And if you don't know how to do that, I'm through with you, Ralph Potts!" Kitty whirled around and stomped off the stage. Potts hurried after her.

When they were gone, everyone turned to Chance for direction.

He sighed. "Maybe we should take a fifteen-minute break." Or a forever break. But he doubted Kitty, Hester, and Mrs. Moody would go along with that.

"I think that's a good idea," Mrs. Moody said. "There are cookies in the Sunday school room." The other adults helped her usher the kids down the aisle. The only person who didn't leave was Hester. He thought she would have something to say about Kitty's outburst or Everly not showing up. Instead, she said something completely unrelated.

"Did anyone tell you how it became a tradition to act out a version of *A Christmas Carol* every year?"

"Mrs. Moody mentioned that the story had been adapted over the years, but she didn't tell me where it all started."

Hester sat down on the carpeted steps that led to the stage, the black skirt of her dress puddled around her like the Wicked Witch of the West after she'd gotten splashed with water. She patted the spot next to her. With no other choice, Chance joined her on the steps. Behind the black netting of her veil her eyes looked even more violet.

"In 1868, a group of people left their homes in the east to come west. Some might've called them adventurers, but the truth was that they were victims—victims of a fractured country, a civil war, and an assassinated president. After losing so many loved ones and dealing with the aftermath of a brutal war, these people wanted to start fresh in a new state that dime novels had glamorized as the Wild West. But when they got to Texas, it wasn't as glamorous as they thought. That first year, every type of calamity you could imagine—tornados, drought, hailstorms, outlaws, and sickness, beset those poor people. A lot of settlers decided they'd made a huge mistake coming to Texas and headed back home. But there were a few strong, determined people who decided to tough it out."

Chance had to wonder what these settlers had to do with Charles Dickens's story and waited for Hester to get to the point. She took her time.

"And things didn't get better. In fact, they got worse. A week before Christmas, the people gathered in the church they had just finished building to discuss leaving Cursed. While they were having their meeting, an ice storm struck. They took it as a sign from God that it was time for them to leave. But with the ice storm raging outside, they couldn't go to their homes and were stuck in the church for the entire night. When the children grew hungry and cold, one of the women pulled out a book and started reading to distract them. The story not only spellbound the children, but also the adults. The following morning the settlers voted unanimously to stay. The book was Charles Dickens's *A Christmas Carol.*"

Chance was more than a little confused. "Exactly how did a story about a selfish, greedy Englishman visited by three ghosts change their minds?"

"Ebenezer could have very easily woken up on Christmas morning and thought it had all been a dream. The spirits were gone. He was alone in his room. He could have ignored the ghosts' lessons and continued to be a selfish, greedy man. But instead, he believed he'd been given a chance to correct the mistakes he'd made and become a better person. He believed in the spirits. But mostly he believed in himself. He believed he could turn his life around and do better."

Hester studied him. "You say you've lost faith in God. But you can't be angry at Him if you don't believe in Him? What you lost was faith in yourself. You lost faith that you could ever be happy again. The settlers lost that faith too . . . until they heard the uplifting story of how a man changed overnight. The ghosts didn't make Ebenezer happy. He did that himself. He had still lost the woman he loved. He still only had one living family member. But it didn't matter. He decided to enjoy what he did have." She smiled.

"Like you, the ghosts made him realize that there were still plenty of things to find joy in."

He couldn't argue. He had found joy again. It had slipped back into his life without him even being aware of it. One minute, he had given up and was allowing himself to drown in a sea of depression. And the next, he was being rescued by a fiery-haired mermaid with amber eyes.

"I'm assuming Everly quit the play because of you," Hester said.

Chance nodded. "We ... formed an attachment. Or at least I did. She doesn't want an attachment. She doesn't think we're a good match. She sees herself as the wicked sinner and me as the pure saint. I told her I was planning on quitting, but she thinks I won't be happy unless I'm preaching."

"Smart woman." Hester's eyes were piercing. "The vision I see—the one I've always seen when I look at you—is of a shepherd with a flock."

"So I just have to learn to live without Everly? Because there's no way she could be a preacher's wife."

She tipped her head. "She thinks that? Or you do?" Before he could get over his stunned shock at her words, she turned to the back of the church. "Oh, good. She came."

Hoping it was Everly, Chance quickly followed her gaze. But it wasn't Everly who stood in the doorway that led to the foyer. It was Paisley. Even though her bruises were gone, she still wore the oversized sunglasses.

"She isn't hiding bruises anymore," Hester said as if reading his thoughts. "She's hiding herself.

But she'll figure it out." She smiled at him. "Just like you will. Now help me up." After he helped her to her feet, she moved down the aisle to greet Paisley. "I'm glad you made it, dear. Henry will be thrilled you're here to watch the dress rehearsal. I'll go get him."

When she was gone, Paisley looked at Chance. "Everly wanted me to tell you to quit calling her. She also said to tell you if you cancel the play because she quit, she's going to kick your butt from one end of Cursed to the other."

"She didn't say butt, did she?"

She smiled. "You know her well. She seems to think that you can find a better Scrooge than a tattooed bartender." She hesitated. "Can you?"

The way she asked the question made him realize that she wasn't just talking about the play. He was sure Everly had told Paisley everything and she was asking what his feelings were.

He shook his head. "No one can replace Everly." And no one ever would.

"Mama!" Henry came hurrying down the aisle with cookie crumbs around his mouth and his long snake tail dragging. He gave his mother a hug before he tipped back his cowboy hat. "Guess what? Aunt Eberly isn't gonna be Cowboy Scooge. And now Pastor Chance has to be him, but Miss Kitty says he can't carry a tune in a bucket so this is gonna be the worst Christmas play eber."

If the dress rehearsal was any indication, Kitty's prediction was right. Chance's singing was horrific. Kitty and Potts still hadn't made up and

Kitty glared at him the entire time, causing Potts to forget his lines. And if Henry wasn't waving at his mother, he was on the floor slithering and hissing and ignoring his cues.

When rehearsal was over and everyone was gone, Chance went around turning off the lights. The last lights he switched off were the Christmas tree lights in the foyer . . . but, strangely, the star on top continued to glow. Which made no sense. The star he'd bought on Amazon had no lights. It was a simple plastic star that had been painted gold. And yet, it appeared to be glowing.

Suddenly, Everly's words came back to him.

*One day, you'll meet a woman who will be perfect for you and you'll get married and have a parsonage filled with little angels who you'll lift up to put stars on your Christmas trees. And don't you dare tell me you don't want that because I see it in your eyes every time you look at Henry. And don't tell me you don't want to be a preacher because I see the same look every time you step up to the pulpit. And you can have it all. The perfect job, the perfect wife, the perfect family.*

Perfect.

The word held so much power for such a small word. Everly's parents had been striving for it. And Chance realized that he had been striving for it too. He'd wanted to be the perfect pastor. Sinless. Godly. More holy than everyone else.

When tragedy hit, he'd realized he was just a human being with all the pain and sorrow and imperfection that goes with it. And yet, he still hung on to that perfect image of what a pastor should be. Which was why he saw himself as unfit to continue pastoring. He wasn't holy enough. And he'd let his insecurities about his righteousness color the way he saw Everly.

Hester was right. He didn't think Everly was saintly enough to be a preacher's wife. He'd pretty much told her exactly that when he'd said he was quitting his job so they could be together. No wonder she had tossed him out on his butt. He had treated her exactly like her parents had—like the imperfect sister. He had made her feel like she would only be good enough for him if he wasn't a pastor, instead of making her feel like she was perfect for him no matter what he decided to do.

And the truth was that Everly would make an amazing pastor's wife. She was kindhearted, talented, and strong. Strong enough not to let a confused and insecure idiot make her feel less than who she was. No one could do that. No one could stifle her light.

Unlike Chance, who had let life stifle his.

As he stared at the star glowing brightly on the top of the tree for no apparent reason, he felt a flicker of something deep inside him. Like a candle flame that had been buffeted by strong winds, but refused to go out. Like a settler who had been stranded in a small church by an ice storm, but refused to give up. Like a man who had lost faith in himself . . . but never God's faith in him.

Right there in front of a star that symbolized faith, love, and hope, Chance knelt to pray.

## Chapter Nineteen

"SO I GUESS you think the silent treatment is going to work." Everly looked across the table at Henry. The kid knew how to glare. She'd give him that. His eyes were narrowed and his chin jutted out. "Well, go ahead and don't talk. Not having to listen to your chattering is a nice reprieve."

"What's a re—" He slammed his mouth closed before he could finish the question.

Everly bit back a smile. "A reprieve is a break from something that's annoying. And your constant chattering can be extremely annoying."

His eyes bugged and she figured his silent treatment was over. "I'm not annoying!" he blurted out. "You're annoying, Aunt Eberly. You gabe away our kittens!"

The sinking feeling she'd been fighting all morning intensified in the pit of her stomach and she had to swallow hard before she could speak. "I didn't give them away yet. Miss Kitty isn't picking them up until Christmas Eve morning to take them to their new home."

"They habe a home! Your home!"

"A room over a bar is not a home, Henry. But when we get to Dallas, I promise we'll find a nice home for you and your mama and me. And once we're settled, I'll get you a cat if you still want one."

"I don't want any old cat. I want Scuttle, Flounder, and Sebastian. And I don't want to mobe to Dallas. I want to stay here in Cursed and be a cowboy!"

Everly started to explain that he could be a cowboy in Dallas, but stopped. Being a cowboy wasn't the only reason Henry wanted to stay. He had gotten attached to the people of Cursed. Hester had become a grandmother to him. Miss Kitty had started him a stamp collection. Otis let him flip pancakes and Thelma gave him extra sprinkles on his donuts. Hayden fixed him Shirley Temples at the bar and told him stories about being a rodeo cowboy. And Chance played Legos with him and told him Bible stories every time he stopped by to talk with Paisley.

Why would a kid want to leave that? And how could Everly take Henry away from it? But she didn't have a choice. She couldn't stay in Cursed. Not when it was a struggle every day to put a smile on her face and try to act like everything was just fine and dandy when it wasn't.

She had fallen for Chance. She had fallen hard. Twice as hard as she had fallen for his brother. But she would get over it. She had to. Breaking it off with Chance was the right thing to do. She wasn't what was best for him. Just like she wasn't what was best for the kittens. Kitty had found them a good home. A home with someone who would be much better at caring for cats than Everly. But she would miss the demons. She would miss them so much.

"And how come you don't want to be Cowboy Scooge?" Henry's sullen voice pulled her out of her depressing thoughts. "Pastor Chance's singing hurts my ears. And if he hurts other people's ears, they might get up and go before it's my turn to sing about Cowboy Scooge shooting a turkey for our Christmas dinner. And it's all your fault!" He crossed his arms and went back to glaring at her.

Everly sighed. "Well, I'm glad you got that off your chest. Now finish your donut, we need to get going."

"Going where? I don't want to go anywhere with a lowdown sidewinder."

She lifted her eyebrows. "I thought you love lowdown sidewinders."

His eyes got all puppy doggish. Which made her think of Chance's eyes whenever she saw him. "Please, Aunt Eberly. Please be Cowboy Scooge. I promise I won't chatter so much and I promise I won't throw any more fits and I promise I will try to say my ba-ba-*b*'s."

It was hard to ignore his plea, but Everly couldn't be in the play. She didn't trust herself to be around Chance and his sad eyes and not do something stupid. Like believe that he really did love her. It had been hard enough ignoring his calls and his visits to the bar. But in her heart of hearts, she knew that she had just been a rebound girl. The girl who made him realize he could be happy again. And he would be.

Once she was gone.

"Are you crying, Aunt Eberly?"

"Not hardly. I just got something in my eye." She brushed the tears from her cheeks before she took out her credit card to pay the bill. "Since you don't want to go with a lowdown sidewinder to the Kingman Ranch, I guess I'll take you back to Hester's."

Henry stared at her. "You're taking me to the Kingman Ranch?" He started bouncing in the booth. "I want to go! I want to go!"

Before they headed to the ranch, Everly swung by to pick up Paisley. She was sitting on the porch with Hester. The two had become close and Everly was thankful to Hester for taking her sister under her wing. Paisley needed a calming grandmother figure as much as Henry did.

As soon as they got out of the car, Henry started excitedly telling Hester about going to the Kingman Ranch.

"What a special treat," Hester said. "The ranch is all decorated for Christmas and the snow will only add to the magic."

While Henry jumped up and down with excitement at the prospect of snow, Everly glanced at the sky. There was a bank of dark clouds on the horizon, but, in Texas, the chances of those clouds producing snow were slim to none.

As if reading her thoughts, Hester spoke. "Things aren't always obvious, Everly. But that doesn't mean they can't happen. Christmas is the time for miracles." For some reason, Everly got the feeling she wasn't just talking about snow. "Y'all have a wonderful time now." Hester smiled at Henry. "And don't eat too many of Potts's sweets. We don't want our Tiny Sidewinder Tim getting sick before tonight's performance."

For someone who hadn't wanted to be in the play, Everly felt a pang of disappointment that she wouldn't be performing with her nephew that night. She hadn't realized how much she'd enjoyed singing and being part of the church group until she'd quit. Maybe when she moved back to Dallas, she would join a choir.

The entire drive to the Kingman Ranch, Henry talked excitedly about horses and cowboys. But he went completely silent when he saw how decked out the castle was for the holidays. There were twinkle lights in all the trees leading up to the castle. When they reached the house, swags of greenery hung over every door and balcony. On the front doors were huge wreaths with festoons of red ribbon intermingled with silver horse ornaments.

The ominous clouds now blocked the sun, causing a drop in temperature. As Everly stepped out of the car, a cold, stiff wind greeted her. She quickly helped Paisley get Henry out of his booster.

Before they reached the doors, they swung open and Shane and Delaney stepped out. They were both dressed in full cowboy garb, with cowboy hats tugged low on their heads—no doubt to impress Henry. Her nephew looked impressed. His eyes widened and his mouth dropped open.

Shane had already met Paisley and Henry, but Delaney hadn't. She smiled and held out a hand to Paisley. "Welcome to the Kingman Ranch, Paisley. I'm Delaney, but you can call me Del." After shaking Paisley's hand, she looked down at Henry. "You must be Henry. I hear you want to be a cowboy."

"Yes, ma'am, I do. And I'm gonna. Hessy says so."

Delaney grinned. "Well, if Hessy says so it must be true." She hooked an arm through Shane's. "And you remember my husband, Shane."

Henry looked up at Shane. "But I thought you were Pastor Chance."

Paisley placed a hand on Henry's shoulder. "Remember Shane and Chance are twins, honey."

"Yeah, but—"

Delaney cut in. "Do you like gingerbread houses, Henry? Our cook, Potts, makes one every Christmas that looks like a miniature Buckinghorse Palace. Come on in and I'll show you."

The castle inside was as festive as outside. In the foyer, a tall Christmas tree had the same ribbon and silver horse ornaments as the wreaths on the door. But it didn't compare in beauty to the gigantic tree in the family room that was decorated from top to full lower branches with heirloom ornaments that had probably been passed down for generations.

"Holy shit!" Henry exclaimed as soon as they

stepped into the room. When everyone turned to him in shock, he shrugged. "But Aunt Eberly says it."

"Gee, thanks for throwing me under the bus, champ," Everly said, as Shane and Delaney struggled not to laugh. Paisley didn't find it amusing. She shot Everly an annoyed look before she scolded Henry.

"I don't care who says it, you don't. Understood?"

"Sorry, Mama. But that's the biggest tree I'be eber seen. And look at all those presents."

"If I'm not mistaken, I think I saw a couple with your name on them," Delaney said.

Henry stared at her. "For me?"

"Yes, sir. I'll be happy to show you. But for now let's go look at that gingerbread castle." Delaney leaned closer to Henry and whispered, "Potts has been a little grumpy because his girlfriend is mad at him so maybe you can cheer him up."

"I can! I'm good at cheering people up. Aunt Eberly was sad because she told Mama she keeps falling for the wrong men and I cheered her—"

Paisley cut in. "That's enough, Henry. I'm sure the Kingmans don't want to hear our life story." She took his hand and sent Everly an apologetic look before she followed Delaney out of the room. Everly started to go with them, but Shane stopped her.

"We need to talk."

She didn't have to ask what he wanted to talk about. "There's nothing to talk about. I'm sure Chance told you everything."

"Not everything."

"Fine. Here's the short version. I pulled another tequila night. Except without the tequila. But this time, I wasn't stupid enough to mistake sex for love. Paisley was wrong. I didn't fall for Chance. I would never fall for someone who is the complete opposite from me. And even though he claims he doesn't want to preach anymore, we both know that eventually he'll change his mind. He's a good man with strong beliefs. He's just been grieving. Which is another reason I would never fall for Chance. I'm not willing to compete with a dead woman."

"There's no competition. Lori was Lori. You are—"

"Nothing like Lori. You told me about how sweet and soft-spoken and . . . perfect she was, Shane. We both know that's not me."

Shane took a deep breath and then released it. "You're right. You're not sweet—but you're kindhearted and loving. You're not soft-spoken—but you're honest and straightforward. As for being perfect, you might not be perfect for some people. But you're perfect for me."

She laughed. "Which is why you chose Delaney."

"I didn't choose Delaney. I choose you."

Okay, this was getting weird. Especially when he took a step closer. His hat shadowed his eyes, but she could feel their intensity. The vibe she was getting wasn't the friendly vibe she was used to.

She held up a hand. "I don't know what's going on here, Shaney, but I feel like I need to make something clear. I'm not still in love with you. I mean I love you as a friend, but that's it. If Delaney getting pregnant has made you feel a little scared and unsure, I get it. But don't let fear cause you to screw up a good thing."

"Why not? You're letting fear screw up a good thing."

She snorted. "Have you ever known me to be scared of anything?"

"You're scared of a lot of things, but usually you don't let your fear stop you. You are one of the strongest, bravest women I know. A woman who has no problem facing her biggest fears." He paused. "Except now. You're running and I'm terrified I won't be able to stop you, Everly."

It was the way he said *Everly* that finally had the truth dawning on her. She grabbed the brim of his cowboy hat and swept it off. Chance's coffee eyes stared back at her. "You . . ." She searched for a name that would fit and could only think of one. "Lowdown sidewinder!"

She turned and walked out of the room. Since she didn't want to ruin Henry's visit to the ranch, she bypassed the kitchen and headed for the door. Paisley would be ticked that she left without her, but she was sure one of the Kingmans would give Paisley and Henry a ride back into town.

Unfortunately, she didn't even make it to her car before Chance caught up with her. "Please, Everly. Just give me a chance to explain."

She whirled on him. "Explain? There is no excuse for what you did. How dare you trick me into coming out to the ranch by using my sweet little nephew. And let me guess, it was Shane's idea. He always loved pulling the twin switch."

"Actually, it was my idea. I love pulling the twin switch as much as my brother. In fact, I used to pull it all the time on Granny Ran and it would make her just as angry as it made you." He grinned. "But that didn't stop me from doing it. I was always a bit of a mischief-maker."

His smile faded. "I forgot that part of myself. Or maybe I pushed it down because it didn't fit my idea of what a pastor should be." He hesitated. "I was trying so hard to be what I thought God wanted me to be that I lost the person He made me. The person who likes the occasional beer and two-stepping and standing up for my brother in a fight . . . and sassy women. After Lori passed, I lost faith. But not in God. I lost faith in myself. I thought I wasn't worthy. But I am worthy. As Granny Ran said, 'God doesn't make mistakes. Only people do.' And I made a big mistake thinking I could be happy doing anything but pastoring. You were right. I don't want to leave Holy Gospel. Or Cursed. It's a good town with good-hearted people who won't hold it against me if I'm not perfect." He pinned her with his brown-eyed gaze. "Because I'm not, Everly. No one is."

"I'm glad you finally figured that out, Preach. Now if you'll excuse me."

He caught her arm. It was freezing cold outside, but the heat of his hand warmed her faster than a blazing fire. "What I'm trying to say is that we're not that different. I'm not a saint. And you're not a sinner. We're just two people trying to do the best that we can."

"Great. Now I'm trying to leave."

His gaze grew intense. "I love you, Everly, and I want you to marry me."

She jerked away from him. "Do I need to slap some sense into you again, Preach? You do not love me and you certainly do not want to marry me. I'm your rebound girl. I get it. After Lori, you wanted to be with someone who was nothing like her. But that's not who you want to spend the rest of your life with."

This time, he took both her arms. "Then I'll tell you who I want to spend the rest of my life with. I want to spend the rest of my life with a courageous woman who refuses to be anyone but who she is. A kindhearted woman who helped rebuild a house and business for two people she didn't even know. A loving woman who refused to separate three sibling kittens. A caring woman who helped a grumpy widower who had given up on life. That's the woman I want by my side for the rest of my life. The woman who will make a perfect preacher's wife. If you want to still manage a bar, that's fine with me. If you want to open up a tattoo parlor, do it. I would never stifle the vibrant, beautiful person you are, Everly. I want to hold you up and let everyone bask in the brilliant light God gave you." He smiled. "The light He gave me. Because without you I never would've found my way back from the dark pit I had fallen into."

Everly tried. She really tried. But there was no way to keep the tears from falling. They leaked from her eyes like a drippy tap. Chance drew her into his arms and held her close. She tried to pull away, but he refused to let her go. Finally, she gave up and sunk into his warm embrace.

"Damn you, Preach. You just had to go and give the best sermon of your life, didn't you?"

His chuckle rumbled beneath her ear. "I have a lot at stake."

She realized that she did too. The rest of her life was at stake. She could continue to push him away. Or she could take a chance. It was as simple as that. She was scared. It was the same fear she'd always had. A fear that she couldn't be what the people she loved wanted her to be. She thought she wasn't a runner. But she'd been running. She'd been running from rejection. Which is why she acted like she didn't care. But she cared. She cared about Paisley and Henry and Shane and all the townsfolk of Cursed. And she cared about a preacher with steamy coffee eyes. It was time to accept that.

It was time to take a Chance.

She drew back. "Fine, I'll stay."

If she had any doubts, they were erased by the look of pure joy on Chance's face . . . and by the kiss he gave her. The man could kiss. This kiss didn't just fill her body with heat. It also filled her heart. She could have continued kissing him forever if something cold hadn't landed on her cheek. She opened her eyes to see white, fluffy flakes drifting down from the sky.

A second later, Henry came charging out of the house.

"It's snowing, Aunt Eberly! It's snowing!"

She and Chance drew back and watched as her nephew jumped around trying to catch snowflakes on his tongue. Before she could warn him to be careful and not trip over the uneven bricks in the pathway, Chance joined him. The two of them jumping around with open mouths and closed eyes had her laughing...and accepting that they were the two boys she loved most in the world.

"So I guess our trick worked."

She turned to see Delaney standing there with a big smile on her face. "I didn't realize you were so devious, Del."

"Then you don't know me very well." Delaney elbowed her in the ribs. "But I think we'll have plenty of time to remedy that."

"You don't mind me moving to Cursed for good?"

"Not at all." Delaney glanced at Chance, who had lifted Henry up to his shoulders. "Looks like you found the right Ransom for you."

# Chapter Twenty

CHANCE WAS A nervous wreck.

Not because of the packed church waiting to witness his horrible acting and singing skills, but because he wasn't sure where he stood with Everly. That morning, she'd said she would stay. But he didn't know exactly what that meant. She would stay in Cursed? She would stay with him? Before he could ask her to clarify, Henry had dragged her to the stables to look at the horses. Then Paisley had gotten worried about driving back to town in the snow. And before he knew it, Everly was gone and he was left feeling scared and unsure of how their story would end.

"There's no need to be scared, Reverend."

Chance stopped pacing and turned to Kitty, who was standing backstage with the rest of the cast members.

"You're just experiencing a little stage fright." Kitty adjusted the holly wreath on her head. "Although maybe it would be a good idea if you spoke the words of the songs, instead of sang them."

"'Cause you can't carry a tune in a bucket!" Henry yelled.

Kitty glanced down at him. "Now, Henry, I don't know where you would get such a thing."

Henry's eyes squinted beneath the brim of his cowboy hat. "But I heard it from you, Miss Kitty. You said—"

Kitty cut him off. "Did you know I brought my mama's brownies for the after party? I bet you could sneak one now if—"

"Don't bribe the child with sugar." Hester walked up in her black dress and spooky veil. Mrs. Moody was with her. "And there's no reason for the reverend to worry." Hester turned to Chance and smiled. "It will all work out."

Mrs. Moody patted his arm. "Of course, it will. Faith, Reverend. Have faith."

Chance wanted to have faith, but if anyone was unpredictable, it was Everly. He thought for sure she would keep the kittens, but she was letting them go. What made him think she would want to keep him? For all he knew, she was packing at that very moment and getting ready to leave town. She certainly wasn't in the audience because he had been checking every two seconds. He was just about to forget the play and head over to Nasty Jack's when a familiar voice spoke behind him.

"Anyone in need of a Cowboy Scrooge that can carry a tune in a bucket?"

Chance whirled to see Everly standing there in a similar costume to what he wore—a solid black western shirt and jeans. Like Chance, her hair had been sprayed white and her face was lined with wrinkles.

She looked stunning.

And annoyed.

"I knew it. You're going to look like a hot Sam Elliott when you get old and I'm going to look like a shriveled old hag."

Relief filled him and he didn't hesitate to walk over and pull her into his arms and kiss her. He didn't know how long they kissed before the three ghosts spoke.

"I told you I was a good matchmaker," Kitty said.

Hester snorted. "You?"

"Of course, me. I was the one who made sure no one tried out for Cowboy Scrooge."

"And I was the one who knew exactly what woman was Chance's perfect match."

"Only because you're a witch."

"Now, ladies," Mrs. Moody cut in. "It doesn't matter how it happened, it just matters that it did."

Chance couldn't have agreed more.

The Christmas musical was a bit of a disaster. Henry kept hissing like a snake whenever he was on stage and drowning out people's lines. Kitty didn't come out when it was her scene and Chance discovered her and Potts kissing backstage. When Chance cleared his throat to get their attention, Kitty drew back and grinned. "You aren't the only one who found love this Christmas season, Reverend. I finally got Potts out of the kitchen." And when it was the Ghost of Christmas Future's scene, Hester went completely off script and took Everly's hand and looked at her palm.

"I see a home covered in so many Christmas lights that it lights up the entire town. In the window, I see a family decorating a tree. The father is holding a little girl up to put a star on the tree while the mother is trying to corral twin boys." Hester lifted her gaze and smiled. "And it can all be yours, Scrooge. All you have to do is believe."

Everly didn't speak for a long moment. Chance figured Hester going off script had made her forget her lines. He started to whisper them to her from backstage when she turned to him and spoke in a clear voice that held no doubt. "Yes, I'll marry you, Preach. But I'm not getting married as fast as the rest of the crazy people in this town and that's final."

Chance didn't wait for the end of the play. He couldn't. He walked right out on stage and kissed her to the loud applause of the audience. When he drew back, she looked at him with dazed golden eyes.

"Fine. I'll marry you whenever you want."

As joy filled Chance at just the thought of making Everly his wife as soon as possible, Tiny Sidewinder Tim took it upon himself to yell his last line.

"God Bless Y'all . . . Eberyone."

Everly had never thought she'd have a fairytale wedding. She hadn't wanted a long white princess dress or a handsome tuxedoed prince or a wedding in a pretty chapel filled with the entire town.

But that's exactly what she got.

And she couldn't have been happier.

"You look like that mermaid princess when she got married on that big boat, Aunt Eberly."

Everly glanced down at Henry in his ring bearer's tuxedo, complete with a cowboy hat. "And you look like the perfect cowboy gentlemen."

"Mama says there's no such thing as perfect."

Everly glanced at Paisley who looked stunning in her red maid of honor's dress. Her bruises on the outside were all gone and the ones on the inside were healing. She had gotten a lawyer, a restraining order, and was working on getting full custody of Henry. She had also started looking for a job. Since Everly didn't want her leaving Cursed, she had offered her a job at Nasty Jack's. Wolfe was all for anything that would allow him to spend more time at the ranch with his wife and daughter.

"Thanks for staying, Paise," she said. "I couldn't have pulled this wedding together so quickly without you."

Paisley smiled and walked over to adjust Everly's veil. "After all you've done for me, it was nice to finally do something for you." She hesitated. "I'm sorry Mama and Daddy didn't come."

At Chance's urging, Everly had called and invited her parents to the wedding. Her mother had declined because of a bad head cold—even though her voice hadn't sounded the least bit congested. Still, it had been nice to reconnect with her parents. She wasn't going to stop calling them or inviting them to visit. Like Paisley said, there was no such thing as perfect. That went for parents too.

"It's okay." She smiled at Paisley and then Henry. "I have all the family I need to see me get wed."

Paisley hugged her tight while Henry wrapped his arms around Everly's legs, his body almost completely engulfed by the full skirt of her dress. "We lobe you, Aunt Eberly. Eben if Mama thinks you're rushing into things."

Everly drew back and looked at her sister. Paisley blushed. "I just want you to be sure."

Everly had spent most of her life being unsure of what she wanted. But she wasn't unsure anymore. Chance's love had made her insecurities vanish and she was able to stop trying so hard not to fit in and accept who she was: A small town girl who had no trouble speaking her mind. A churchgoing woman who enjoyed singing in Christmas musicals. A damn good manager of the best honky-tonk in Texas. A sister and aunt who loved her family. And a preacher's woman who didn't want to wait a second longer to claim her man.

She nodded. "I'm positive."

The Christmas Eve service made for a breathtaking wedding. The entire Holy Gospel church was filled with flickering candlelight. A friend of Chance's from seminary school officiated. Chance stood next to Shane in a western-cut tux and black Stetson. When Everly headed down the aisle toward him, his face told her everything she needed to know.

She was the woman he wanted to spend the rest of his life with.

The ceremony went off without a hitch . . . until it was Chance's turn to repeat his vows. Since he had repeated them dozens of times when officiating weddings, she was surprised when he stumbled over the words. Of course, she couldn't let it slide. She planned to spend her life teasing her husband.

"Spit it out, Preach. People are waiting to party."

The partying took place at the Kingman Ranch. With all the trees and the entire castle lit up with Christmas lights and snow still clinging to the north-facing turrets, it looked like a magical fairytale castle. The inside was just as magical. The huge tree in the family room was lit and a fire blazed in the fireplace and a delicious spread of food filled the counters and table in the kitchen, along with plenty of Gretchen's pies. The Kingmans were all there, including Danny, Teddy, and Maribelle. When Gretchen placed a sweet little Maribelle in her arms, Everly couldn't help thinking of her own babies.

The kittens were gone. Kitty had come and picked them up that morning to take them to their new home. Everly didn't realize how much she loved the little demons until they weren't there to torment her anymore.

"Something wrong?" Chance asked.

"I was just thinking about the kittens. What if Kitty was wrong about the people she gave them to? What if they won't figure out that Flounder likes her cat food softened with a little water and Scuttle needs lots of toys to keep him occupied and Sebastian only sleeps well on a pillow?"

"Stop worrying. I'm sure they'll be purr-fect parents."

She sent him an annoyed look. "Just so you know, Preach, I'm not a person who finds puns funny."

"That's too bad because I happen to be a very 'punny' person."

She rolled her eyes. "Stop or I'm going to have our marriage annulled."

"Sorry, babe, but you're stuck with me." His coffee eyes twinkling. "Like superglue. Now stop worrying about the kittens. Like three wise ghosts once told me, 'No need to be scared. It will all work out. You just have to have faith.'"

Everly tried. She really tried. But faith was Chance's strong suit, not hers. After they'd cut the Chocolate Candy Cane Surprise Pie and started dancing, she couldn't keep her feelings in another second.

"I made a mistake!"

Chance stopped waltzing and stared at her. "A mistake? You don't want to be married?"

She shook her head. "Not about marrying you. That's the best decision I've made my entire life. I made a mistake about getting rid of the kittens. We need to get them back."

Chance smiled. "Then it's a good thing I know exactly where they are."

Once they'd thanked their guests and the Kingmans for a beautiful reception, they headed back to Cursed. But by the time they reached the *Welcome to Cursed* sign, Everly started to feel guilty.

"What if the kittens are Christmas gifts from Santa for three sweet little kids who will be completely disappointed if kittens aren't under their tree? Hester predicted that they would be with three children."

Chance reached over and took her hand. "They're not gifts for kids." He turned onto the street where the parsonage was.

"What are you doing? Are the kittens with one of your neighbors?"

"I thought we should change first. We don't want to knock on someone's door in a tux and wedding gown."

When he pulled into the driveway, Everly was shocked speechless. The house was covered in so many Christmas lights it lit up the entire neighborhood. There were lights along the eaves and rooftop and more lights covered the trees and bushes. A nativity scene sat in the front yard with a big lit-up star over the manger.

"Nice job, Sparky," Everly said when Chance came around to open her door.

He laughed. "You don't know how accurate that is. I almost slid off the roof when I was stapling the lights to the peak." He glanced back at the house. "But it was worth it. I love Christmas. It's my favorite holiday."

"You could've fooled me, Preach."

He winked as he helped her out of the truck. "That's the point. I didn't fool you."

When they got to the door, he opened it and then lifted her into his arms. As he carried her over the threshold, she realized she shouldn't be thinking about kittens. She should be thinking about the man who had changed her life forever. They could get other cats. They *would* get other cats. And maybe a dog or two. She had always liked dogs. And a horse. If Henry was going to be a cowboy, he needed a horse.

She looped her arms around Chance's neck and kissed his cheek. "I love you, Preach."

He stopped in the living room and set her on her feet. "I love you too." He kissed her, the kind of kiss that gave a glimpse of years and years of love and happiness. When Everly was just starting to think about peeling off his sexy tux and enjoying the body beneath, the sound of breaking glass drew her attention.

"What was that?"

Chance cringed. "I'd say it was a broken ornament."

She stepped back and looked at the tree. Sure enough, a broken Santa ornament lay in pieces on the floor beneath. "But how did it fall when we were standing clear over—" She cut off when a cute little tiger-striped face peeked out from beneath the tree.

"Flounder?" She hurried over and knelt by the tree. The kitten pounced out, followed by two other furry demons. "Scuttle! Sebastian!" She scooped all three kittens into her arms and pressed her face into their soft fur before she looked up at Chance. "You got them back. You got my kittens back."

Chance smiled down at her. "I didn't get them back. I was the home Kitty found. I knew you loved the kittens. You just needed to realize how much."

She should be angry at his deception, but how could she be angry with him for knowing her better than she knew herself. She set the kittens down and got to her feet. Tears welled in her eyes, but she didn't care. Chance had proven he was a man she could trust with her tears. "Thank you. I couldn't have asked for a better Christmas present."

He pulled her into his arms. "Nor could I." He kissed her. When he drew back, he glanced at the window and smiled. "Look, it's snowing again."

She turned and saw large flakes drifting past the window. As Chance pulled her closer and they looked at the beautiful lights of the Christmas tree with the backdrop of falling snow, she remembered what Paisley had told Henry about there being no such thing as perfect.

At this moment, she had to disagree.

This was perfect.

She knew there would be plenty of tough times ahead. But there would also be plenty of moments like this one. And maybe that's what life was ... perfect imperfection.

Chance tipped his head and whispered in her ear. "Merry Christmas, Everly James Ransom."

She smiled with her heart. "Merry Christmas, Preach."

## THE END

*Turn the page for a special*
SNEAK PEEK
*of the next Kingman Ranch novel.*

# SNEAK PEEK!
## *Charming a Cowboy King,*
*coming March 2023!*

---

"LOVE POTION PIE? Now that's a pie I'll have to try." The trucker driver in the grease-stained ball cap winked flirtatiously. "Of course, I'm already half in love."

It took every speck of willpower Paisley Grayson Stanford had not to snort in disgust. She wasn't disgusted with the flirting trucker as much as the entire concept of love. At one time, she'd believed in fairytales and happy endings, but not anymore. Love was for naïve fools and Paisley was through being a fool.

Completely ignoring the trucker's comment, she pasted on a smile and repeated the order. "That's two Coors beers and two slices of Love Potion Pie. I'll have that right out." She turned and headed toward the bar that covered one entire wall of Nasty Jack's. Multi-colored Christmas lights hung above it year round, but tonight, there was also a long banner of pink paper hearts and red cupids. Below the banner, cuddling couples whispered sweet nothings to each other as they enjoyed their drinks and pie. At the end of the bar, a group of cowboys had congregated around the redheaded bartender.

Stepping up to the bar, Paisley watched as her sister efficiently filled beer glasses . . . while putting the cowboys in their place. Unlike Paisley, Everly had no problem dealing with men.

"Don't complain to me about not having sweethearts on Valentine's Day. There are plenty of women in this bar who would love to spend the night two-stepping with a handsome cowboy. Now stop standing here wasting your time with a happily married woman and get to asking. Or am I going to have to stop serving you gutless wienies beer and start serving you Shirley Temples." The cowboys looked thoroughly chastised, and as soon as they got their beers, they slunk off.

Everly walk over to Paisley and rolled her eyes. "Men. They complain about not being able to get a woman when they're not willing to make the effort it takes to get one. Even your four-year-old son has more guts." A smile spread over her face. "I guess Henry told you about Brooklyn Ann 'the prettiest girl eber.'"

Paisley laughed at her sister's impersonation of her son. Henry still struggled to pronounce his *v*'s. "Who's Brooklyn Ann?"

"I guess she's a pretty little blond he met in his preschool class. He sweet talked me into buying him the biggest Valentine card at Cursed Market to give to her."

Henry hadn't said a word about the card or the little girl. Paisley couldn't help feeling hurt. She had always been good at hiding her emotions, but Everly knew her too well.

"Now don't get upset, Paise. It's not a big deal. What kid wants to talk to their mother about girls?"

Paisley set her tray on the bar. "He doesn't talk to me about anything."

"Now I find that hard to believe." Everly started taking clean glasses out of the dishwasher and putting them on the shelves behind the bar. "Your son is the biggest chatterbox this side of the Pecos."

"With everyone but me. I get the feeling he doesn't even like being around me. I get it. Lately, I haven't been what you'd call fun."

"Now stop it," Everly said. "Henry adores you. And you're fun. You've just had a lot on your plate recently."

That was putting it mildly. Paisley plate was heaped so high she couldn't see around it. And if not for her sister's help, things would be even worse. She couldn't thank Everly enough for all she'd done for her. Not only had Everly taken them in when they first arrived in Cursed, but she had also found them a place to live and given Paisley a job and watched Henry while Paisley was dealing with the train wreck her life had become.

But in the process, Paisley felt like Everly had replaced her in Henry's heart. And why wouldn't her son like Everly better? She was vivacious, risk-taker, and fun while Paisley had always been subdued, a rule follower, and boring. Which probably explained her nickname in high school. Dull Barbie. She might be pretty, but there was nothing but air behind the fake plastic smile.

And she still used that fake smile to hide her true feelings.

"You're right. I'm sure Henry will tell me about Brooklyn Ann and the Valentine's card as soon as he wakes up tomorrow. When he got home from preschool today, we didn't have much time to talk before I had to come to work."

"You could've come in late, Paise."

She shook her head. "No. You've taken over for me enough. Especially since you're still a newlywed." She glanced around. "Where is Chance? I thought for sure he'd be here tonight."

A dopey look came over Everly's face. "Chance and I celebrated Valentine's Day this morning. Although I think he has something up his pastor's sleeve for tonight. I found a grocery receipt in his pants pocket when I was doing the laundry for steaks, wine, strawberries, and whip cream. So I figure he's planning a special late-night dinner when I get home." Her eyes twinkled. "And, hopefully, some naughty sex. When I married a preacher, I never thought he would be so good in bed. Did I tell you about the thing he did the other night with his tongue?"

Thankfully, before Paisley had to endure her sister's graphic details, Kitty Carson yelled out from down the bar. Kitty delivered the mail and gossip to the townsfolk of Cursed, Texas. She had a head of stiff red hair and a voice that could be heard in three counties.

"Everly! Can I get another margarita? Potts says he only drinks beer, but when I came back from the ladies room my drink was suspiciously gone and his kisses taste like tequila and lime." She leaned over the bar more. "Hey, Paisley! An official-looking package arrived for you right before I closed up the post office tonight. I'll bring it by the Malones' house first thing tomorrow morning."

Paisley felt all the blood drain from her face. She knew what was inside the package. While a part of her was happy her nightmare marriage was almost over, there was another part of her that mourned the loss of all her hopes and dreams.

"A margarita is coming right up, Kitty," Everly's voice cut into Paisley's thoughts. "I'll make one for Potts too." As she pulled two margarita glasses from the dishwasher, her gaze caught Paisley's. "You okay?"

She wasn't okay. How could a person be okay when they had finally realized that their life had been nothing but smoke and mirrors? But she wasn't about to tell her newly married sister that.

"I'm fine. I better get two bottles of Coors and two slices of Love Potion Pie back to those truckers."

Everly set down the margarita glasses and pulled two beers out of the cooler. Once they were opened, she set them on Paisley's tray. Her eyes held compassion. "Look, I get that you have an aversion to men after what happened to you. But I think it's time you got over that and started taking your own food orders to the kitchen. I hired you as a waitress and that includes working with the cook—even if you don't particularly like him. So, like I told those cowboys, stop being a wienie and face your fears."

As much as Paisley wanted to argue, she couldn't. Not only because she hated confrontation, but also because Everly was right. She shouldn't expect her sister to run the bar and take orders back to the kitchen. It was Paisley's job and she needed to stop being a wienie and do it.

Leaving her tray on the bar, she headed to the swinging door that led to the kitchen. She hesitated for only a second before she pushed her way through. The kitchen smelled like a mixture of sautéing onions, frying French fries, and spicy wings.

The person responsible for those smells stood at the cooktop with his back to Paisley.

Hayden West.

Just the sight of him had Paisley's stomach tightening.

To say Hayden rattled her was an understatement. Every time he was near, she felt unnerved and jumpy. She didn't understand why. He had never been rude to her. In fact, he was almost overly polite. While he joked and teased with Everly, he spoke to Paisley like she was his Sunday school teacher. Although she doubted he had spent much time in Sunday school.

From what Everly had told her, Hayden was an ex-bronc rider from Montana who started drifting around the country after his rodeo career cratered. He'd wandered into Cursed by accident and decided to stay a while. During the day, he worked as a ranch hand for the Kingman Ranch, and four nights a week, he ran the kitchen at Nasty Jack's. He was good-looking, but not so much that it was intimidating.

And maybe it wasn't his looks as much as his size that unnerved her. He stood well over six feet with broad linebacker shoulders and biceps that stretched out the sleeves of the T-shirts he always wore.

Right now he was wearing a Nasty Jack's shirt that hugged his back muscles like a second skin. His faded blue jeans weren't tight, but they fit well enough to show off the curves of his butt. Whenever Hayden stepped out of the kitchen, every woman in the bar stopped what she was doing to watch the copper-stitched wrangler pockets pass.

Every woman, except Paisley. She wasn't interested in men's butts. Or men in general. Everly was right. After what she'd been through, she did have an aversion to men.

"Mrs. Stanford?"

She lifted her gaze from Hayden's butt to find him looking at her over one linebacker shoulder. Steam rose around him from whatever he was grilling on the cooktop, causing his dark walnut-colored hair to curl around his ears and forehead in thick, wavy strands. He had obviously caught her checking his butt out, but his pale blue eyes didn't hold a twinkle of cockiness. Nor did his wide mouth tremble with a suppressed smirk. His eyes held the same look they always did when he looked at her.

Sympathy.

It was that sympathy, coupled with the way he rattled her, that caused her dislike of the man. She didn't need anyone's sympathy. Especially a saddle tramp's.

"I need two slices of Love Potion Pie," she said in the snappish voice that always came out of her mouth when she spoke to Hayden.

He didn't seem to take offense. Which annoyed her. While her stomach felt like it was filled with Mexican jumping beans, Hayden remained calm and collected.

"Yes, ma'am." After wiping his hands on the dishtowel tuck into his jeans, he moved to the prep island where a cluster of pies sat. Wolfe Kingman owned Nasty Jack's and his wife, Gretchen, made all the pies from scratch. Besides beer and margaritas, they were the bestsellers at the bar. People came from all over Texas to get a slice of Gretchen's pies.

With an efficiency that was surprising for a man with such large hands, Hayden sliced into the tower of toasted merengue covering the top of the pie and plated a slice. Beneath the thick merengue was a layer of dark chocolate custard on top of an even darker chocolate crust.

"I think I might like this pie better than the chocolate peppermint pie Gretchen made for Christmas," he said without looking up. "Have you tasted it?"

"I don't like chocolate."

He hesitated for a brief second before he sliced another piece of pie. "I don't think I've ever met a woman who didn't like chocolate." He picked up a bottle of chocolate syrup and drizzled it over the top of each slice. "So what is your favorite pie?"

"I don't have a favorite. I don't like sweets."

His gaze finally lifted and his eyes held surprise. "No peanut butter cookies, coconut cake, apple pie, strawberry shortcake?" When she shook her head, he looked completely confused. "Ice cream?"

"No."

He looked at her as if she was a puzzle he couldn't quite figure out. Or a weird anomaly that made no sense. "Not even candy as a kid?"

"We weren't allowed to eat candy."

Again, she saw sympathy before he looked away. "Smart parents. I spent a lot of time at the dentist because of my love of candy and sweets." He picked up the plates of pie and moved toward her. Try as she might, she couldn't stop herself from stepping back.

He froze. His gaze locked with hers for a long, uncomfortable moment before he turned and set the plates back on the prep island.

"I'll just let you get those. I need to check on my hamburger sliders before they get too well done."

Relieved, Paisley quickly grabbed the plates and headed for the door. But before she could get there, Hayden stopped her.

"Paisley."

It was the first time he had used her given name. For some reason, hearing it spoken in his gravelly voice made her feel even more unnerved.

She gripped the cold plates and tried to keep her voice steady and calm. "Yes?"

After a long, uncomfortable silence, he finally spoke. "I get why you're leery of men, but I just want you to know that I would never hurt you."

© Charming a Cowboy King excerpt by Katie Lane

## PREORDER TODAY!
*https://www.amazon.com/dp/B0BM3WGNZW/*

# Other Titles by Katie Lane

Be sure to check out all of Katie Lane's novels!
*www.katielanebooks.com*

**Kingman Ranch Series**
Charming a Texas Beast
Charming a Knight in Cowboy Boots
Charming a Big Bad Texan
Charming a Fairytale Cowboy
Charming a Texas Prince
Charming a Christmas Texan
Charming a Cowboy King (March 2023)

**Bad Boy Ranch Series**
Taming a Texas Bad Boy
Taming a Texas Rebel
Taming a Texas Charmer
Taming a Texas Heartbreaker
Taming a Texas Devil
Taming a Texas Rascal
Taming a Texas Tease
Taming a Texas Christmas Cowboy

**Brides of Bliss Texas Series**
Spring Texas Bride
Summer Texas Bride
Autumn Texas Bride
Christmas Texas Bride

**Tender Heart Texas Series**
Falling for Tender Heart
Falling Head Over Boots
Falling for a Texas Hellion
Falling for a Cowboy's Smile
Falling for a Christmas Cowboy

**Deep in the Heart of Texas Series**
Going Cowboy Crazy
Make Mine a Bad Boy
Catch Me a Cowboy
Trouble in Texas
Flirting with Texas
A Match Made in Texas
The Last Cowboy in Texas
My Big Fat Texas Wedding

**Overnight Billionaires Series**
A Billionaire Between the Sheets
A Billionaire After Dark
Waking up with a Billionaire

**Hunk for the Holidays Series**
Hunk for the Holidays
Ring in the Holidays
Unwrapped

# About the Author

KATIE LANE IS a firm believer that love conquers all and laughter is the best medicine. Which is why you'll find plenty of humor and happily-ever-afters in her contemporary and western contemporary romance novels. A USA Today Bestselling Author, she has written numerous series, including *Deep in the Heart of Texas, Hunk for the Holidays, Overnight Billionaires, Tender Heart Texas, The Brides of Bliss Texas, Bad Boy Ranch,* and *Kingman Ranch*. Katie lives in Albuquerque, New Mexico, and when she's not writing, she enjoys reading, eating chocolate (dark, please), and snuggling with her high school sweetheart and Cairn Terrier, Roo.

For more on her writing life or just to chat, check out Katie here:
Facebook *www.facebook.com/katielaneauthor*
Instagram *www.instagram.com/katielanebooks*

And for information on upcoming releases and great giveaways, be sure to sign up for her mailing list at *www.katielanebooks.com*!

Printed in Great Britain
by Amazon